UNPREDICTABLE
COMBINATIONS

TIA DORÉ

Published by

**GENERAL STORE
PUBLISHING HOUSE**

499 O'Brien Rd., Box 415,
Renfrew, Ontario, Canada
K7V 4A6
Telephone (613) 432-7697 or 1-800-465-6072
www.gsph.com

ISBN 1-897113-05-6
Printed and bound in Canada

Cover design, formatting and printing by
Custom Printers of Renfrew Ltd.

Library and Archives Canada Cataloguing in Publication

Doré, Tia
Unpredictable combinations / Tia Doré.

ISBN 1-897113-05-6

I. Title.

PS8607.O74U66 2004   C813'.6   C2004-906073-2

UNPREDICTABLE COMBINATIONS

BY TIA DORÉ

To Mary

Thank you for being
here tonight & enjoy
the book.

Tia Doré

2005

Chapter 1

Martha lay half-asleep. All that kept her remotely awake was her husband Hank firmly implanted in her, humping away. As usual it made no difference to him if she was awake or semi-conscious from exhaustion. It was a nightly ritual, which she escaped only when he was too drunk to care. The late news played on the twelve-inch black and white TV in their room. The small set projected multi shades of grey as the modest television flashed images of the day's news.

A little piece of her brain connected to the winning lottery numbers being announced: "2 - 11 - 16 - 17 - 21 . . ."

True to form, Hank grunted a premature ejaculation. After he withdrew from her she thankfully turned on her side and dozed off, but not before being treated to the sound of him farting his last gas of the day and cracking every joint in his body.

Martha dug her head deeper into her pillow. The numbers she was able to hear over his grunting did sound familiar, but after playing the lottery for so many years, they always seemed to ring a bell. Slumber beckoned her to dreamland with the promise of sweet escape. She'd check the results in the morning.

Martha awoke at her accustomed punctual 5:00 a.m. It was a long commute to her waitress job across town. Martha enjoyed the early morning best; it gave her an opportunity to sit quietly sipping her coffee while listening to the radio before life set in. Still in her bathrobe, she reached up to the top of the fridge to turn on an old turquoise and white GE radio with a large, round, luminous dial. She still recalled when she and her mother had gone to get it.

Her mother had stuffed several stamp booklets into her purse. She clutched it tightly while riding the bus to the redemption centre as if carrying something of great value, all the while holding Martha's small hand. Patiently they stood in line with others holding their withered and dog-eared stamp booklets. One man in front of them held a brown cord-handled bag, booklets stacked within. Martha stood wide-eyed in wonder at the fortune within. What was he going to redeem them for? Surely something of great value! When his turn arrived, the man requested the catalogue's colour TV, and a murmur spread through the people in line waiting their turn. It took both girls at the counter several minutes to verify his stamp books.

Martha's mom finally got to redeem her booklets for the radio. On their way out, they paused to watch two men loading a large cardboard and wood box into the back of a station wagon while its proud new owner looked on.

It was a rare, happy moment when they arrived home with it. Her father looked at the radio with admiration; he placed it with reverence atop the fridge where it still sat today.

Something kept nagging at her subconscious, but Martha could not put her finger on it. Once her coffee was ready, she sat at the old Formica-topped dinette set to sip it quietly. The radio broadcasted the news with the usual reports of fires, murders, robberies, politics, and world affairs. Following a few jingle-filled commercials came the weather, and finally the winning lottery numbers: 2 - 11 - 16 - 17 - 21 and 35.

The familiarity of the numbers caused Martha to feel an unpleasant flutter in her chest that bordered on a seizure. Her head spun with the tunnel vision associated with a panic attack. Reaching for her glossy black vinyl handbag, she dug into the zippered side compartment where she kept her ticket. She pulled it out, and, holding it before her, scrutinized it: *2 - 11 - 16 - 17 - 21 and 35!*

There they were, the same numbers she had just heard on the radio! In her excitement she had missed hearing the size of the jackpot. With the two-by-three-inch red-bordered ticket clutched tightly in her trembling hand, the room spun harder and her heart raced faster. She read and reread the numbers. For years she had played the same combination, more out of habit than hope.

Her parents had faithfully played the weekly lottery without ever winning. The practice was so automatic she never gave any thought to actually winning; even worse, she had no idea of what size the jackpot was. Over and over again she reread the numbers. Maybe she had misunderstood? No, she was certain she had heard correctly. Millions? No, certainly not, but it had to be a considerable amount. She knew she'd have to share the jackpot with other winners, but surely it would give her at least a few tens of thousands. There she sat, her hand to her forehead, elbow on the table, sitting in a stupor, staring at her ticket to freedom.

"HEY!" Hank's familiar growl grounded her as he lumbered into the kitchen pointing at Martha sitting at her mother-in-law's cast-off Formica and aluminum table. The way Hank stood in the middle of their kitchen, scratching the crevice between his penis and testicles, he appeared far older than his thirty-seven years.

"How many times do I have to tell you to keep that fuckin' radio low." Reaching up to his receding coif with the same hand he had just removed from his groin, he waved off a few unruly wisps of hair impeding his view. Martha couldn't help wondering why he always smelled the same way— the perfect anti-libido, a blend of sweat and urine residue. With the habit of years of diplomatically giving in to his every whim, Martha quickly replaced the ticket back in her purse, clasping it shut. He belted out a rancid belch; the stench crept across the modest kitchen.

"Want a coffee, honey?" Martha asked dutifully.

"Naw, I'm going back to bed. Just keep it quiet." A fart resonated from the hall as he departed.

"I'm taking the car to work today, sweetheart," Martha informed him.

Hank's bare footfalls stopped, and he reappeared in the doorway. "You don't drive two blocks across anything with a median, and now you're telling me you're going to drive across town on your own?"

It was true. Martha had been a nervous driver forever, and had never mustered enough courage to drive through the neighbourhood's highway perimeter unless she was accompanied by another driver. Martha quickly countered his observation.

"The news just said the bus drivers may stage a walkout at noon, and I don't want to get caught across town. I won't be back in time to prepare dinner."

There would be people to see and plans to make. They lived in a Canadian province where community property ruled, and she had no intention of handing over half her winnings to a squandering husband.

Hank frowned in consideration of what she just told him, "Yeah? Well, just bring the car back full," he said, disappearing once again.

Monday 9:08 a.m.

Helen Zupinsky had just sat down at her desk when the phone rang.
"Marion Lloyd, attorney at law, good morning."
"Lloyd, please," A man's voice asked.
"He's not in yet, may I take a message?" she dutifully asked.
"Yes, actually you may. Tell him it's Phil Rogers. Just let him know I got the court ruling, and he can kiss my ass and my business goodbye," he informed her.
"Oh, will you be making your ten o'clock appointment, Mr. Rogers?" she naively asked.
His reply came after a long pause. "I don't think so," he simply said before rudely hanging up.

Martha nervously thumbed the frayed Yellow Pages in a phone booth at a truck stop diner a few blocks from her house. She strained to find an attorney's name in the midst of the dust, fumes, and noise from the many rigs pulling in and out of the parking lot. Finally she found the listing for attorneys. Unfortunately only a half page remained of the category; the rest had been ripped out. She ran her finger down the page; her choices were limited to barely a few intact listings. One stood out:
Marion Lloyd
Attorney at law
Divorces / Civil Suits
Injury claims
1818 Capital St.
(502) 555–1212
She was pleased by the fact it was a woman. She was certain that a peer would have a better understanding of her motives. She promptly dialed the number.

Helen Zupinsky, with raised eyebrows and pursed lips, opened Mr. Lloyd's appointment book and scratched out Mr. Roger's appointment. Helen was an elderly, matronly woman who was old-fashioned and unfamiliar with today's business environment. A widow for the past four years, she had restarted working after her husband of forty-eight years passed away suddenly. She wasn't doing it for the money; rather, she did it to maintain contact with the world and other people, and to maintain her sanity. Alone at home she would only dwell on what was and wonder why her Walter had to go.

Just then, Helen was interrupted by the phone ringing.

"Marion Lloyd, attorney at law. May I help you?" She politely answered.

Martha responded anxiously, "Yes, hello. I'd like to make an appointment."

Helen responded, "Certainly. I can fit you in around the end of this—"

"It's very urgent, I'd need something sooner if it's possible," Martha interrupted.

Helen said, "Can you be here within an hour? I happen to have a cancella—"

"YES, yes, I can, thank you! Where on Capital Street are you?" Martha asked exuberantly.

"Just East of Morgan. Your name is?"

"Martha Kowalski . . . It's regarding a divorce," she said anxiously.

Just then, Martha heard a loud rapping sound that echoed in the phone booth.

"Hey, Lady, you gonna be long?"

Martha turned to see a large, burly, cigar-chewing, unshaven truck driver. His pot belly was pressed against the folding glass door. She stared at him in surprise.

"Well? Are you?" He repeated.

Hurriedly she ripped the page with the lawyer's coordinates and bade farewell to the secretary who had so graciously squeezed her in. Accidentally dropping the receiver, she dashed past the rude driver, being careful not to touch him.

Martha showed up at her appointment just in time. Nervously she had navigated the downtown streets heavy with early morning rush-hour traffic. Breathlessly she announced her arrival to Helen, who informed her that it wouldn't be too long.

Moments later, the secretary called out, "Mrs. Kowalski, Mr. Lloyd will see you now."

The name "Mr. Lloyd" didn't ring a bell right away, and Martha just sat there staring into space.

"Ms. Kowalski . . ." The round secretary pointed her glare over her horn-rimmed glasses at her as her outstretched hand directed her towards the lawyer's door.

"Oh, yes." Martha rose, trying not to look too confused while making her way through the indicated door.

Martha realized the lawyer whose name she had pulled from the Yellow Pages was a man. Suddenly she felt exposed and vulnerable. She'd had the preconceived notion that she would be relating her unfortunate situation to a woman. It never dawned on her to ask a man for help.

She reluctantly entered the room where Mr. Lloyd was feigning involvement in paperwork. The familiar racing forms that had adorned her kitchen table every weekend for the past seventeen years didn't escape her notice as he slipped them into the top right-hand drawer of his desk.

Dusty files were stacked in careful piles, but didn't show signs of recent activity. Lloyd's desk was also littered with menus, indistinguishable files, and various papers. In fact, Martha didn't really care what he was or wasn't up to. All she needed to hear was that there was hope for a carefree future; and be given the permission to practice legalized self-indulgence.

"Mr. Lloyd?" she shyly asked.

"Yes. Call me Marion, please." He replied in a distracted manner, barely making eye contact. He directed her to sit. Martha took her place in a chair before him and addressed him across his messy desk. Marion Lloyd leaned forward, straining to hear her as she recounted her reasons for being there. It was a story he had heard many times before: deadbeat husband . . . working two jobs to support him . . . he gambled, he cheated, verbally and physically abused her, drank, swore, stank, spit . . . *Yeah, yeah, go on*, he thought while he stifled a yawn. Lloyd made a futile attempt to camouflage the inconsiderate gesture, but his flaring nostrils betrayed him.

Martha, far from being a confident woman, took his involuntary indiscretion as a sign that this was a bad idea. After all, he was a man, and her life experience had proved that men were scum and not to be trusted. Yet here she was asking one for help! She would prefer talking to a woman, but then she realized that a woman attempting to help another woman—other than washing dishes—was futile in a man's world.

She shifted uncomfortably in her chair, again reflecting that this was a bad idea. Marion picked up on this.

Attempting to put her at ease, he said, "Mrs. Kowalski, can I offer you a coffee?"

Surprised by his offer, Martha's attention was refocused on him. "Oh, my, no thank you, I couldn't."

The suggestion that a man would serve her was so alien to her she actually blushed at the suggestion.

"I just brewed a pot. It's no bother. I'll join you."

He picked up his mug and spun around in his chair to face a small credenza behind him where a Proctor Silex brewing machine sat. He unceremoniously blew dust off a mug and poured them two cups. He thought about what she had been telling him and quickly categorized her as a "Wanna." *I wanna divorce, but as shitty a life as I have, I don't have the balls to change it. Here's another cocksucking bitch who has no idea what she fuckin' wants. All she knows is that what little she has she doesn't want to lose.*

He turned and set the cup before her. "How do you take it?"

"Oh, black is fine," she blushingly said.

"Are you sure?" holding up the powdered cream and sugar.

"Well, maybe just a bit of each."

She took both containers from him and daintily scooped four sugars into her cup before topping it off with a copious amount of whitener. Shyly she blushed and smiled as she stirred the thick mixture.

"The house is in both your names?" he asked.

"Oh no, the house is his father's. You see, we inherited it from my mother, but he had me transfer ownership to my father-in-law."

He raised an eyebrow, "Why would you do that?"

"Well, you see, he told me we'd pay less taxes that way."

Lloyd sat stunned. This woman would have to study to be as dumb as a doorknob, he thought. As the conversation went on, he slumped in his chair, recapping things in his mind with a finger to his temple, a look of bewilderment displayed on his face. No money, nothing belongs to her, zero self-esteem. Even the ill-fitting clothes she wore were probably hand-me-downs. This bitch had nothing. The prospect of a profitable new case quickly faded. He wouldn't be surprised if this woman pulled out a glass jar full of pennies to pay him.

He looked up at the wall clock behind her. The track would open in twenty minutes and he was sitting on a sure thing. He stood up and interrupted her.

"Mrs. Kowalski, I empathize with you, but from what I understand, unless you're willing to part with all your worldly possessions and pretty well start from scratch, there isn't much I can do for you. Now as far as my fee goes I'm willing to waive it, but if you wish to pursue this further I'll have to charge you from this point. I hope—"

She cut him off. "Fine."

Caught off guard he asked, "Excuse me?"

"Fine, no problem, I had every intention of paying you," she declared.

"I'm afraid my fee is one hundred and fifty dollars per hour, Mrs. Kowalski," he sternly pointed out.

"If that's what it is, then I'm fine with it. Can we please continue, Mr. Lloyd?"

He slowly sat down, unsure of the turn of events, his cockiness cut down a notch.

Martha sat straight, her hands on her lap clutching the patent leather purse firmly, and launched into a tirade.

"Mr. Lloyd, I was raised a strict Catholic. The women in my family pretty well were all uneducated and obedient. All the way back to my great-grandmother, I watched the women in my family beaten, abused, and lowered to a level of submissiveness that I had accepted as the norm for marriage and the lot of women in general. All of the women in my life married men that abused them not only physically, but mentally as well. When I was a young girl my poor mother instilled in me the morals she was brought up with: find a man, marry young, serve him, and raise a family. 'Don't look further than the kitchen,' was what she always told me. I loathed my life and am now in a position to change it. I won't be denied that opportunity. Can I count on you, or not?"

Lloyd almost involuntarily nodded in agreement. Promptly she rose, greeted him farewell, took one of his cards from the desktop, and informed him she would be in touch. After leaving, she strode out of the building, not stopping until she was around the corner and certain to be out of view from Lloyd's office. Then she leaned against a red brick wall, feeling faint and out of breath. Once she regained her composure, she left for her next intended destination; a step that would lead to one of the biggest mistakes of her life.

Chapter 2

Marion Lloyd brushed off his meeting with Martha Kowalski. After all, he was late for his appointment at the track. Briskly he walked out of his office and past his bifocaled secretary.

"Are you going out?" She cried out louder than she intended. "You have an appointment with Mr. Collins from the bank."

"Yeah, yeah, tell him I'm in court and to wait if he wants," he replied, walking into the hall clutching his racing forms.

Once in his neglected Volkswagen, he cranked the engine, and it reluctantly turned over before sending the car lurching forward, leaving a puff of blue smoke where it had been parked. Marion merged into the boulevard traffic, driving in automatic mode. He made a daily pilgrimage to the racetrack, which was intentionally only half a mile from his office, in order to bet on a few of the races. He preferred the daytime betting; the entourage was more professional, less touristy. Nobody wasted his time by hemming and hawing at the betting window, or chatting up the teller. Before he knew it—and incapable of saying how he had gotten there—he had arrived, parked his car, and was walking briskly towards the track. His car was still sputtering and running on as he began to run towards the building. Without a second to spare he entered and placed his bet.

"Five hundred on Mudder Earth in the First," he panted, slapping cash on the counter.

Retrieving his betting slip, he headed for the stands. Thankfully his preferred aisle seat was unoccupied. There were all the familiar faces. The old man in his eighties with his worn straw fedora, chewing on the butt of his familiar cigar (come to think of it, Marion never noticed him lighting it). Down the row from him was the weaselly, greasy-haired, nervous, suit-wearing man who by the looks of it was surely a sales rep of some sort. A cell phone always rang in his pocket but he never answered it. In front of him, two rows down, was the dishevelled man who always smelled of alcohol and perspiration. Although it was a cool summer morning, the man appeared to be sweating.

"AND THEY'RE OFF!"

The horses burst out of the gate. Mudder Earth was in front from the outset, and maintained a lead of a length or so. Into the first turn, a horse from mid-pack seemed to have a burst of energy and was gradually moving up. Mudder Earth was maintaining a steady, powerful stride. There was barely any movement in the positions well into the turn except for Mudder Earth losing ground to that other horse moving up inch by inch.

Marion was fixated on the race, much like most of the spectators except for the drunk who threw his papers to the floor and stomped away, seemingly on the verge of crying. With a trembling bottom lip he rushed up the steps past Marion, leaving a whiff of malodorous air in his wake. Obviously his pick didn't have a chance.

Mudder Earth was overtaken in the final turn by the other horse and most of the pack. In the last stretch, Mudder Earth was almost dead last and didn't even show. "Fuck!" Marion voiced almost inaudibly.

Leaving, he dumped the paper's racing section in a trash bin, and made his way past the betting windows. In the parking lot, the drunk was soliciting handouts. Marion made an effort to avoid him. He heard sob stories all day long; he wasn't in the mood for another one. He quickened his pace and skirted the man by walking down the next aisle. Finally in his car, he paused for a moment to analyze what had just happened. He had lost another bundle of cash. His bank manager was probably already sitting in his office waiting to discuss his loan situation. The landlord gave him till next week to come up with the back rent on his office, or he was out, and a similar situation was happening with his apartment. Worse still, he had owed money to Vincent, a local bookie, for a college game gone bad, for two weeks now. He decided to call his secretary and tell her he was delayed in court.

Bill Collins sat in Lloyd's dreary waiting room impatiently; his appointment was twenty-seven minutes ago. He knew that because he'd checked his watch at least twenty-seven times since then. He often looked up over the top of the old magazines he kept flipping through to occasionally spy on Lloyd's secretary. He noted that the phone hadn't rung once since he had arrived. The secretary nervously fidgeted and seemed uneasy. Although she had been typing almost continuously since his arrival he doubted the sincerity of her actions. She was typing non-stop without pausing to look at any document. The rapping of the keys was incessant and annoying. And by God, who still uses a typewriter these days?

Helen eagerly picked up the phone before the first ring had subsided. "Marion Lloyd's office, attorney at law. May I help you?" She dutifully answered.

"Is he there?"

"Yes."

"Don't let him know it's me," Marion ordered.

"But . . ." she managed to say before Lloyd interrupted her.

"Tell him my assistant called to say I'd be held up in court all day and to call me tomorrow," he instructed.

"Yes, certainly, I'll let him know," she replied before replacing the handset in a motion that seemed to take forever.

"Mr. Lloyd will be . . ."

Angrily Collins discarded the magazine and stood up before she could finish the sentence. Helen clasped her hands nervously upon her desk and braced herself for the tirade she was sure would come.

Collins, red-faced and frowning, growled, "Tell him it's over. He'll understand." With that he turned and walked out.

The slamming of the door confirmed his anger. The plate glass framed in the door rattled precariously. Helen wondered how such seemingly fragile glass could stand all the slamming it had been subjected to over the years and still be intact.

Calmly she turned, pulled out the paper covered in gibberish from the typewriter, and disposed of it in the wastebasket.

Monday 10:44 a.m.

Martha nervously navigated the city streets looking for the address she had been given. Since she was too nervous to safely drive and scout for the building, she had decided to park and to find it on foot. She finally spotted it:

LOTTERY OFFICE

Parking the car, she nervously retrieved the only quarter she had in her purse. With trembling hands she fed the meter with it and noted the thirty-minute time limit. Hoping it would be enough, she briskly walked up the building steps. Once inside, a security guard directed her to the office she sought. She was surprised to find that it was laid out much like a bank. An armed guard stood by the door while half a dozen people processed transactions behind the counter. She took her place in line, waiting her turn. Everyone who left was smiling; obviously they were winners who had collected their proceeds. Most were accompanied. Martha seemed to be the only one alone.

Her turn finally came. She nervously stepped up to the window. Tunnel vision overwhelmed her; all sound seemed to be obliterated. A loud ringing sound resonated in her head. She addressed the young man across the counter from her. Her voice sounded distant and distorted to her. In a barely audible voice, she said, "I believe I won some money."

"Ticket, please," he simply said.

She slid the crumpled stub of paper across the Arborite counter top. He took the slip. Quietly he viewed his computer screen. Without turning his head, he briefly gazed at her, studying her momentarily. He then picked up his phone and dialed an extension.

"Yes . . . one of the jackpots is here," he said, and hung up. He placed the ticket on the counter and weighted it down with his stapler. Dutifully he informed her that it would be a moment. His face devoid of expression, he took a step back and clasped his hands behind his back, standing seemingly at attention.

Suddenly Martha's tunnel vision dissipated and she became alert, panic welling up in her. "Is there a problem, sir?"

"No, ma'am, it'll just be a moment," he calmly said. His look seemed to become a stare of resentment and envy.

From the corner of her eye she spotted a heavyset, balding older man exiting a glass office and walking towards their window. From behind the partitioned counter he signalled the guard over. He made eye contact with the young man who indicated the ticket on the counter. Without acknowledging poor Martha, he picked up the slip and held it up to the screen. His eyes scanned both the ticket and the screen before finally turning to Martha, saying,

"Madam, please follow the gentleman behind you to my office."

"But that's my ticket! I bought it Friday at Willowvale convenience—"

"I have no doubt, Madam. Please come to my office," he calmly restated with a glint of amusement in his eye.

Martha turned to see the towering black man in uniform beckoning her to follow him. She nervously followed the guard. The older man unlocked the heavy glass partition leading to his office, before beckoning her to enter. The guard closed the door once she was safely inside before resuming his post.

"I'm Paul Rudgard, lottery office supervisor," he informed her, offering his hand.

Martha extended hers; Paul Rudgard felt her hand tremble. He held onto her hand and kindly put his arm around her shoulder before leading her to a chair. With a gentle pressure, he urged her to sit. A young lady joined them and sat cross-legged next to his desk with a clipboard and pen in hand. Somehow she resembled him—the same kind eyes.

He slid the ticket towards the young lady, whom he introduced as Karen Ross, explaining that she would witness the proceedings and take notes. She smiled at Martha and took the ticket, verified the numbers, then asked Martha to sign the back of the ticket. She slid it into an official-looking envelope, clipped it to her board, and left the room.

Paul leaned back in his high-back chair.

"Karen will be just a moment; would you like a coffee?"

Martha shook her head nervously and croaked,

"Water, please."

Her mouth and throat were dry. Paul jumped to his feet.

"Of course!"

He grabbed the insulated water container on his desk and poured water into a Styrofoam cup. Martha gulped it down and wordlessly held her cup out with a trembling hand for more. Paul poured out another cup, and finally a third, before she finally said that she was fine, thank you.

Silently they sat for a moment before she finally asked,

"Did I win?"

Paul raised his eyebrows and leaned forward.

"Yes, it appears you did. We're just waiting for official confirmation, which should come momentarily."

Martha knew she had all the numbers, but an amount hadn't formed in her mind. She sat quietly clutching her purse, feeling awkward in the glass-walled office; all eyes seemed to be on her.

"How much did I win?" she finally asked.

"Once it's confirmed, it looks like approximately a little over eight and a half million dollars."

The number barely registered before she lost consciousness.

Monday 11:02 a.m.

Hank Kowalski sat at The Lightning Bar, sipping his third beer. The barman Phil was drying some glasses, preparing for the midday customers, while "You picked a fine time to leave me, Lucille" played on the radio. Hank made it his daily routine to go to the bar and hang out for a few hours. It was his version of networking; you never knew who might feed him a lead on an interesting job. What Hank considered interesting was something with a good salary, preferably a supervisory position with reasonable hours, maybe something part-time that would not interfere with his schedule. And he wanted something close to home.

He found that all the good jobs went to the wrong people. His game plan was to be available when a job worthy of his "savoir faire" came along. He had his ears and eyes open; not to worry, Hank had a handle on things.

"Well if it ain't Hank Kowalski!" a sultry woman's voice sounded from the doorway.

He turned to see Jackie a.k.a. "just call me Jack Daniels." She staggered towards him, having obviously gotten an early start on her drinking. She sauntered up to the stool next to him and sat. Her large, pendulous breasts spilled over the top of her low-cut blouse as she provocatively leaned against Hank's arm. Her ridiculously short skirt rode up on her hefty buttocks as she tried to steady herself on the vinyl-upholstered stool. Her tight clothes showed off her layered belly. She gave Hank a long, wet kiss on the lips before saying teasingly,

"Hey, Hank, buy a girl a drink?"

Hank signalled the bartender, who served up her regular—a Jack Daniels on ice, of course. She downed the drink in one gulp.

"So Hank, talk to me," she decreed.

He filled her in on his plans and such, justifying his leisurely life as simply being between career decisions at the time. He quickly turned the question to her. She coyly giggled and leaned her head on his shoulder, almost falling off her stool in the process. Hank reacted quickly, grabbing her arm and left breast in an attempt to steady her. She looked down at his hand before gazing back up at him.

"Squeezing the produce before buying, Hank?"

He removed his hand and blushed. She cackled loudly before taking his hand and sliding it into her top.

"C'mon, Hank, I'm just teasing—you know what's mine is yours."

He squeezed her large breast, grinning before removing his hand when the bartender gave him a frown.

"Still married, Hank?" giving him an innocent little-girl look.

"Yep. She's off working, though."

"You know, Hank, if I had a man like you at home, I'd never leave the house."

Hank grinned at the compliment.

"Well, maybe we can play house a little bit," winking at her.

She accepted his offer by squeezing his groin for support and sliding off her stool. Hank paid the bar bill and followed her out.

Hank sat on the couch, his pants down around his ankles as Jackie blew him. Her hefty breasts rested on his thighs; he watched her platinum-blonde head with its salt and pepper roots bobbing in his lap. She wasn't half as pretty as she thought she was, but man could she suck. He closed his eyes. He had fucked her once before in the back of the pool hall some time ago. Actually, he had banged her with a bunch of other guys when she made some sort of stupid bet over a hockey game. She said she'd fuck all of them if the home team lost, as long as they paid her bar bill that night. The home team won, but she let them fuck her anyway.

The men split her fifty-three-dollar bar bill, and Paul Henderson ran to the local pharmacy to pick up a box of condoms while Jackie was taking a leak. Being regular customers, it was an easy task convincing the owner to allow them access to the back room for their little escapade. Paul returned quickly and divided the package of condoms. As the men argued about the accounting of the cost of the prophylactics compared to the amount of the bar bill, Jackie staggered into the storage room. Her skirt was hiked up around her waist.

"Ready, boys?" she asked, seemingly not fully conscious.

Paul took her in his arms and kissed her, and she willingly allowed him free access to her attributes. They all stood with their condom in hand waiting for their turn. Jackie and Paul staggered over to a stack of beer cases piled in the corner. She allowed him to prop her up onto them as she unbuckled his belt and released his cock. She skillfully slipped the rubber on him before spreading her legs wide. Paul entered her in one svelte thrust. He aggressively fucked her till he came. Once he withdrew another man quickly took his place. Hank was third or fourth in line and as drunk as everyone else. He had managed to get it up but fell victim to the pressure of the men waiting their turn. He finally had to concede defeat and forfeit his moment of pleasure. After the others finished he was too impaired to go for seconds, and besides Jackie at that point had passed out cold.

Now he was getting it back; she was an expert cocksucker. She got him hard enough to perform but not too aroused so he'd blow his load. She tore a condom package using one free hand and her teeth. Sucked the rubber into her mouth and applied it deftly onto his ready cock. She then mounted him. They had barely started fucking when the phone started ringing.

DRING!

They both ignored it; Hank was thrusting in her as she humped him in return.

DRING!

Their copulating picked up speed.

DRING!

Hank's breathing increased; Jackie started moaning.

DRING!

The interruption was starting to irritate Hank, and Jackie complicated things by ordering him to ignore it.

DRING!

He lifted her up and laid her on the couch, where he rammed her mercilessly.

DRING!

She urged him to fuck her harder.

DRING!

She yelled out that she was coming and ordered him not to stop.

DRING!

But the phone took its toll, rendering him soft.

DRING!

Jackie felt him going flaccid in her and stared up at him in disbelief. "You fucker, don't do this to me!" she yelled.

DRING!

His flaccid cock plopped out of her. She yelled, "You asshole, I don't fuckin' believe it!" pushing him off her onto the floor.

DRING!

"Wait, don't go!" He yelled after her, but she was already out the door staggering down the cracked cement walk, her shoes clasped in one hand, suggesting he go fuck himself.

"Hello?"

Whoever it was had hung up. He slammed down the receiver, swearing.

Not receiving an answer, Paul Rudgard hung up, and dialed a number from a business card he also had found in Martha's purse. It appeared to be an attorney.

Monday 11:07 a.m.

Marion Lloyd raised his cell phone when it rang. Seeing that it was his office, he decided to ignore it and let it go to his voice mail; he was on his way to the office anyway. It rang again, then again while parking his car. When it rang for the third time he answered, "WHAT?"

"Mr. Lloyd, there's an urgent message, it's from the lottery office and they're asking you to contact them immediately," his secretary blurted.

"Who? . . . What the fuck are you talking about?" he shouted into the phone.

"Apparently someone you may know is there. They want you to call them right away—they say it's urgent."

He jotted down the name and number. He contemplated the message for a moment before crumpling it up and tossing it out his side window, certain it was either a crank call or a mistake. Rolling up his window, he stepped out of the car. Walking to his building's rear entrance, he noticed the piece of discarded paper rolling along the pavement past him propelled along by a light breeze. He observed it stop against the doorway; it seemed to be taunting him. He stooped down to pick it up, and impatiently smoothed it to look at the information again. Frowning, he punched in the number.

Marion impatiently waited for his call to be answered. He was about to sign off on the fifth ring when a young woman finally answered,

"Good morning, Provincial Lottery office."

Marion, still skeptical, asked for Paul Rudgard. He held while his call was being transferred.

"Paul Rudgard speaking."

"Yes, hello, my name is Lloyd. Apparently you called my office."

"Yes, I did. Thank you for calling back so quickly. We have someone here you may know. We didn't know who else to call—your card was found in her purse when she fainted."

"Fainted? Who?" Marion questioned.

"Her name is Martha Kowalski."

"Martha Kowalski!" Lloyd repeated. "Yes, I know her. What's this about?"

"Come down to our office and we'll discuss the situation. We're located at 575 Fifteenth Avenue, Suite 101. How fast can you get here?" Paul asked.

"Ten minutes," Lloyd informed him. Signing off, he returned to his car, and in his rush to exit the parking lot he impatiently gunned the engine, narrowly missing a collision with a cyclist.

Lloyd was true to his word, arriving ten minutes later. An ambulance marked his destination. Finding a parking spot around the corner he ran to the building, bolting past two good-humoured paramedics who were casually leaving, one pushing an empty stretcher and another one toting an emergency pack. A security guard waved him in and escorted him once he identified himself. He was led to the glass-enclosed office where Martha Kowalski sat pale and slumped in a chair surrounded by three women, one of whom was applying a cold compress to her forehead.

"What happened?" he asked, perplexed.

Rudgard, standing behind his desk, hands on his hips, informed Marion that not knowing who the woman was, they were at a loss as to whom to inform. Besides her I.D. and his card, they had found nothing else.

The lawyer said, "What's she doing here?"

"Maybe it's best if she tells you," Paul answered.

Marion separated the women surrounding Martha. Her slitted eyes saw Marion, then opened wide in surprise.

"Mr. Lloyd! What are you doing here?"

"I wish I knew, Mrs. Kowalski," he replied.

She tried to stand but was persuaded to remain sitting. At that moment, Karen returned, confirming the authenticity of the ticket, and slipping Paul a sheet of paper.

"Mrs. Kowalski, we owe you a cheque. Karen, please draw it up," Paul instructed.

Marion, holding her hand, asked with all the sincerity he could muster, "Why are you here, Mrs. Kowalski? What's going on?"

Shaking her head she managed a confused response

"I'm not sure now. I won some money, it seems. A lot of money. Is that right, Mr. Rudgard?"

Paul was still standing behind his desk, the paper Karen had handed him in one hand, the other in his pocket. He glanced warily at Marion before raising the paper to glance at it. He directed his answer to Martha.

"Exactly eight million, six hundred and fifty two thousand, four hundred and six dollars . . . twenty-six cents."

Raising his eyes, Marion stared back at him. Slack-jawed and incredulous, Marion grasped the arm of Martha's chair to steady himself.

Paul continued, "We'll need your signature on some documents and pictures taken for the media—"

"No pictures! And absolutely no publicity." Marion stood up, dropping Martha's hand and taking a step towards Paul. "As Mrs. Kowalski's attorney I will not allow it, and I request reviewing any document she is to sign."

Paul raised his eyebrows. "The pictures are optional, Mr. Lloyd; however, her name will be released to the press—"

"No, No! Absolutely not, that's unacceptable!"

Calmly Paul leaned forward and rested his outstretched arms onto his desk, addressing Marion with a determined gaze and authoritarian voice.

"Under the terms of the lottery office and provincial law, all winners' names must be divulged to the public. A picture must be taken, again for public record; however, release of it to the media is optional. That is the way it is."

Marion conceded to Paul's authority, and all proceeded to get through the red tape involved. Martha signed whatever Marion okayed, and she posed for the obligatory photo of her holding the cheque that would totally change her life forever. Once it was all done, congratulations and handshakes were exchanged all around and Martha and Marion left the building.

Chapter 3

It had become a spectacularly beautiful day; the sun shone bright and strong, not a cloud impeding its glory. The coolness of the late spring morning had dissipated and been replaced by a warm, calm breeze. Martha paused on the building steps momentarily, raising her face to the afternoon sun, taking in the glorious warmth while removing her overcoat. Marion noticed some pleasant features as the sunlight lit up her overly pale complexion. For a woman without a speck of makeup she could look worse, he thought.

She took in a deep breath and opened her eyes. As she exhaled she looked at Marion, who was staring.

"What now?" she asked.

"Well, let's grab a bite and we can continue our conversation of this morning," he suggested.

"Oh, the conversation you cut short because I was wasting my time and yours? No, thank you."

Martha folded her coat over her arm, and turned and walked towards her car with determination. Marion quickly pursued her, asking her to wait. Martha maintained a steady stride, head held high, as she strode confidently towards her parking place, Marion trying to keep pace.

Stopping suddenly, Martha exclaimed, "Shit! They towed my car!" She spun to look up and down the street, trying to spot her car.

Marion seized the opportunity to offer her a lift, but not before offering lunch. Martha reluctantly accepted. They found a small bistro restaurant across from the lottery office. Martha felt very out of place, seated at a table being served instead of serving. Nervously she clutched her purse, which contained the cheque. Marion tried to put her at ease by teasing her about worrying about a car that she could buy with just one day's interest on the money she now had. However, she didn't comprehend his meaning, and gave him an impatient look.

"Do you have any idea what's involved with that much money? Considering the fact that it's a lottery win, at that," he asked while studying the menu.

"What do you mean?" she asked.

"Well, first of all, your husband would be entitled to half that money in a divorce. And your attitudes of being emotionally attached to old wrecks like your car, brown bagging lunches, cutting coupons, and vacationing at the park should be a thing of the past. People are going to come out of the woodwork trying to sell you swampland in Florida, houses, cars, vacations, condos. Charities will be hitting on you for everything you can imagine: cancer, diabetes, AIDS, ingrown toenails. Religious fanatics, you name it—and it's going to start tomorrow as soon as your name is printed in the paper. Get ready for marriage proposals, people wanting to adopt you, people looking for jobs. Trust me, the phone is going to ring off the hook."

Incredulously Martha listened to his tirade with her mouth agape. "What am I supposed to do?"

"If what you told me this morning is sincere, divorcing your husband will be the first step. Unless he's a total idiot he's going to hit you for half, but if you stay with him he'll probably drink half of it and beat you till he's got the other half. Next you will need an entourage."

Martha cocked her head. "Entourage?"

"Professional people who can manage your money, accountants, investment counsellors, personal secretary, butler, maid . . ."

"And a lawyer, I suppose?" she interrupted sarcastically.

"Yes, absolutely a lawyer," Marion responded, without missing a beat.

"You, I suppose?" Martha added dryly.

"I could, yes. As a matter of fact you should start by putting the funds from that cheque in a safe place. We'll eat and then I'll drive you to my bank."

"I agree, but it'll be *my* bank."

Marion could see that this beaten, domesticated woman had decided to take control of her life, but she was going about it like a bull in a china shop. She seemed determined to do it the way she never could: her way. They both ordered. Marion chose the ribs with a Guinness and an entrée of calamari. He always lived his life as if the big payoff were right around the corner (or in this case, right across the table). Martha ordered a chicken salad sandwich, toasted, and the water was just fine, thank you. She, too, lived her life as always, reading menus from right to left.

While awaiting their meal, Martha excused herself.

"I've got to make a phone call."

Marion reached over and grabbed her arm rudely. He quickly released it and apologized when he realized the harshness of his move. "I'm sorry . . . a phone call?" he inquired.

"Yes, to my employer." She innocently replied.

"Employer!" he exclaimed. "You don't want to do that." He smiled ironically.

"But—"

Marion raised his hand. Bewildered, he said, "Martha, you don't want to leave a trail of breadcrumbs at this point—please sit."

He took a moment to gather his thoughts before continuing, while she sat back down.

"Martha, are you afraid he'll fire you?" He paused in order to let her absorb the sarcastic question. "You have to step cautiously from this point on. Please let me help you."

She lowered her eyes, blushing at her naiveté as she conceded to his logic.

They barely spoke during the meal. Both were pensive. Throughout her whole life, Martha had never had two dimes to rub together. All of a sudden she was in a position of finally breaking free from Hank. However, she cringed at the thought of having to part with half her fortune. Suddenly half of eight point six million didn't seem enough. She must find a way to keep it all after twelve years of work, sweat, and tears. This on top of the physical and mental abuse he had heaped on her, as she had constantly been bombarded by his foul body odor, washed his stained underwear, and endured bad sex. She'd be damned if she'd split the money. She would not pay to be rid of that man.

Marion in the meantime ate quietly, contemplating the bizarre turn of events. A few hours ago, a simple-minded, belittled woman sat in his office, trying to free herself of a pitiful husband and life. Then suddenly he was sitting across the table from a simple-minded, belittled multi-millionaire. He looked at her; she ate with her head bowed, taking tiny, inconspicuous bites. She had absolutely no idea of the fortune she had won or what to do with it. Maybe she'd buy better perfume, comfortable shoes, maybe a new car—maybe she'd spring for a mid-size, *Yeah, a*

Buick, maybe, why not? He couldn't help but feel that money was wasted on the foolish ones. Had he won that money, boy he'd really live, the best of everything, women, champagne, cars, travel, a little gaming. He pictured himself sitting in the roped-off area of the casino reserved for big rollers. That would be sweet.

They passed on the coffee and dessert, opting to move on their plan of depositing the cheque. Martha climbed into Marion's car. She was surprised to find that, as bad as her car was, it was still better than this.

Marty Fitz was pissed off. There was once a time when this country was great. He recalled when people took pride in their job, when people would put in a full honest day's work. Milk would be on the doorstep by six in the morning; by seven, the neighbourhood would be buzzing with activity. Fathers and husbands heading off to work; children skipping off to school; buses, trains, trucks already crowding the city. He remembered when a full day's wage was paid for a full day's work. Not like now when a man doesn't see his mail before noon.

Since his traditional wake-up time of ten, Marty had already checked his mailbox several times. His welfare cheque was already one day late; he was certain it would be there today, if only that fuckin' unionized prick of a mailman would move his ass. He'd been tapped out for a week now, living on leftovers and beer. Hard liquor, his beverage of choice, had run out a while back, so that he had to resort to the only affordable option he had—ale. Unfortunately, beer is not as good an anaesthetic as liquor and would interrupt his much-needed sleep with frequent trips to the washroom. However, anything was better than full consciousness, which would expose him to the pain in his back that had sidelined him over twenty years ago after a forklift accident. He found that alcohol was far more effective than those damn pills he'd been prescribed; but then again, it never stopped him from opting for a combination of both.

Cheque in hand, Marty turned the corner on Main Street from Gunn Avenue. In a moment of distraction, and annoyed by the bright sunlight, he stepped off the curb and was promptly honked at by a swerving Cadillac. After giving the motorist the finger he staggered through the intersection on his way to the bank three blocks down. Once inside he found a line of about half a dozen or so people waiting their turn.

He spotted Martha Kowalski, Hank's wife. She was standing off to the side with a tall man in a dark suit. He observed as Phillips, the bank manager—whom Marty knew well from his many rejected loan applications—stepped out from his office and greeted them both. Martha introduced him as Marion Lloyd. Marion! Must be a fag, dressed like he is, and carrying a girl's name. In the twenty minutes or so of waiting time he watched between small forward steps as the line advanced like molasses on a winter's morning. Both Martha and the slicker took a seat in Phillips' office. Hank was nowhere to be seen; maybe she was with a relative taking care of a loan, an inheritance, or something. Then again, why wasn't Hank there? Marty knew he wasn't working.

Phillips sat slightly slumped in his high-backed chair with both arms resting on the chair's armrests listening to the man talking. Martha sat quietly, her head pivoting from one to the other like a spectator at a tennis game. After a moment or so, Phillips sat up and leaned forward resting his elbows on his desk. With his head cocked to one side and a puzzled look on his face he seemed to be straining to hear. At one point his jaw dropped and he quickly turned his head to Martha. She unclasped her purse, which she had been tightly clutching in her lap, and retrieved an envelope.

Phillips accepted it from her, and proceeded to open the flap, pulling out the contents that appeared to be a cheque. Phillips slumped back into his chair, his hand to his forehead. He reached across his desk to depress an intercom button. Marty heard a discreet buzz from behind the teller's glass.

"Yes, Mr. Phillips?" the young woman behind the glass said.

"Jill, please come into my office," said Phillips.

"Yes, Mr. Phillips, I'll just finish with my—"

"No, Jill, *now* please. Get one of the other girls to finish for you."

Jill did as she was told.

Marty rolled his eyes, certain that whatever she had to do that was so urgent was going to slow things down even further. Phillips was closing the vertical blinds in his office window when Jill walked in, obstructing Marty's view. He eventually had his turn; he smacked his lips and fidgeted nervously while the teller counted out his money. In short order, he was finally on his way and went directly to his favorite haunt. He was going to catch up on the latest news, maybe shoot a game or two of pool, and then he'd pick up some TV dinners, snacks, as well as an assortment of beverages, before heading home.

It was now mid-afternoon, and the place had started attracting a few early birds for happy hour. He walked up to the bar and cheerfully ordered a scotch on the rocks. Usually he didn't like his liquor diluted, but damn! was it hot outside. He downed the first in one gulp and, grimacing, signalled the bartender for another. Only once his glass was full again did he take the time to scan the bar.

It took a little focusing in the dim lighting before he spotted Hank sitting in a booth towards the back of the bar. Hank had returned after his little incident with Jackie. Marty slithered off the stool and made his way towards him. Halfway there, he loudly announced himself with a, "Hey, Hank, it's been a while!"

Hank smirked when he saw Marty; being seen with a drunk was never good for networking, hampering his chances of scoring work. He'd humour him till someone else came in that he could join, and then dump this boozer.

"Just saw the little lady at the bank," he blurted, taking a seat across from Hank.

With an unimpressed look, Hank downed his drink again.

"Martha? Naw, can't be—she's working 'cross town, she's not due for her evening shift at the plant till seven."

"Well I know Martha when I see her, and she was in Phillips' office with some guy in a suit discussing something, figured you'd know."

Hank looked at him blankly, not sure what the old man had seen. As far as he was concerned, he could have confused her for someone else, maybe even confused the day he saw her.

"All I can say is, whatever they were there for, it turned the place upside down, place was buzzing like a beehive. People walking in and out of Phillips' office, phones ringing, passing each other slips and forms. I tell you, never seen nothin' like it."

Hank rubbed his chin contemplating the information while staring skeptically back at Marty. Then he stepped over to the public phone on the wall between the Men's and the Ladies'. He dropped a quarter into the slot before dialing a number. After speaking to someone for about a minute, he unceremoniously slammed the phone back on the hook, dropped a bill on the bar, and stormed out.

Marion and Martha were just wrapping up their business at the bank. A temporary account had been opened. A cash advance of ten thousand dollars was given for now and a credit card application filed. They were to return later in the week to finalize some details, but for now at least the money was secured and at an interest rate a few points above the current rate, which had been negotiated by Marion, giving Martha a daily return of just under two thousand dollars. It would do till they could find a good investment counsellor to diversify the money.

They both thanked Mr. Phillips and the staff before making their way out of the now empty bank. It was three-thirty and the bank had closed half an hour ago. They exited the bank by the back door, which led into the alley parking lot. At that very moment Hank rapped on the bank's front door. Mr. Phillips walked to the front of the bank to investigate the knock. He saw Hank looking into the bank's foyer, his hands shielding his face from the bright sun's glare. Phillips waved his arms motioning the bank was closed. Hank shouted something through the door. Phillips approached him.

"Phillips, was my wife here today?" Hank demanded.

Phillips heard the question, but had been cautioned by Martha to keep the day's dealings confidential. He motioned to his ear indicating he couldn't hear, mouthing the word "closed" before turning and walking away. In the interim, Marion pulled out of the alleyway, stopping not ten feet from where Hank was standing, before merging into the boulevard traffic. Neither party noticed the other.

Martha felt relieved the money was out of her purse and safely deposited. She still held the deposit slip she had been given showing the amount. Now that she had a moment to think, the day's events started to hit her and she felt a panic attack welling up; her brow was covered with perspiration and her breathing increased to a rapid pant. Marion turned to see her distress and asked if she was all right, but her only response was to cover her face with her hands and cry uncontrollably. He pulled over to put his arm around her to comfort her. He held her and whispered that all would be okay. Once he managed to comfort her, he wiped her tears away with his thumb.

"I've got the perfect solution," he stated before putting the car in gear again.

His words of encouragement comforted Martha as she began to relax. She asked where they were going and what she should do now. His only response was that first she was going to do something therapeutic and then they would discuss things over supper. When he said *supper*, panic struck her.

"Supper! Oh my God, Hank will be expecting me home soon," she exclaimed.

Irritated, Marion replied, "So what? Fuck him! This morning you wanted to be rid of him, now you're worried if he's going to go hungry. Right now your biggest problem is focusing on your life from this day on. The only thing you can't afford is going home so he could beat, or maybe even kill you."

She sat quietly looking out her side window, her eyes unfocused, reflecting not on her future, but on letting go of her past. She knew Marion was right.

Marion pulled into the Westhill Galleria parking lot. Martha looked at him, puzzled, her eyes asking what they were doing there.

"You need some shopping therapy. Come on, let's go," he declared.

"But this place is exp—" she stopped herself before completing the ridiculous statement when Marion turned to look at her in exasperation.

She let him lead the way; their first stop was an upscale women's boutique. A tall, slim older woman stood cross-armed next to the counter situated in the middle of the store. Her expression showed revulsion at what she saw walking in. Marion, thankfully, was dressed sharply in his suit. Regardless of his precarious financial situation, he always dressed to impress.

He stepped up to the woman, looked her in the eye challengingly, and simply said, "Dress her, elegantly casual for now. Price is no object."

The woman nodded compliantly, and wordlessly approached Martha. With subdued aversion, she stood behind Martha and peeled off her antiquated overcoat. For the next hour and a half Martha was dressed, re-dressed, accessorized and displayed for Marion, who sat in the comfortably upholstered mahogany chair across from the dressing rooms. Martha was given no options. He sternly declared that tomorrow was hers, but today her ass was his. Her comments and opinions regarding availability of bigger pockets or flowered patterns were ignored. The saleswoman kept putting together stylish, elegant outfits for her. All Marion did was nod in agreement, or shake his head if he didn't like something in particular.

When Martha was given an assortment of undergarments to try, Marion's first sexual thoughts for Martha surfaced. At one point, Martha partially opened the cabin door to ask the woman something while wearing only a satin bra and panties. Her figure was trim and taut from years of hard work; her legs seemed muscular and well defined in spite of the fact that her calves were overdeveloped. Her stomach was flat and firm and her breasts were copious. The full-length mirror behind her reflected firm, trim buttocks cradled within the satin panties.

Marion was pleased at her seemingly keen interest in improving herself, but her ease at adapting stopped short when Martha was shown handbags. She categorically refused to consider changing her handbag, pulling it away from the stunned saleswoman when she reached for it. The woman stepped back in surprise at her response. Martha stared at her defiantly. Marion quickly rose to put his arm around Martha's shoulders to calm her down. He recognized her reluctance to change it, concluding that her emotional response was due to the effects of "too much, too soon." He apologetically suggested to the clerk that the handbags would have to wait for another time.

Once the clothing was decided on and the sale tabulated, four large bags were deposited before them upon the counter.

"Four thousand, three hundred seventeen dollars, and six cents. What card will that be charged on, sir?" the pretentious saleswoman asked.

His only response was "Cash." Pointing a finger at Martha, who was now decked out in a designer blouse and skirt, complete with matching scarf and shoes, complemented by a frayed old black handbag. A look of total astonishment was reflected on the woman's face as Martha sheepishly pulled out a ludicrously thick envelope and counted out the money. As they left the store, the still puzzled woman called after them, indicating Martha's old clothes left lying on the counter.

"Madam, your clothes!"

Without turning, Marion shot back, "Burn them!"

They had a quick bite before leaving the shopping centre. Afterwards, they strolled back to Marion's car. Once again, Marion had to admire Martha's figure as she tried cramming the day's purchases into the cluttered trunk of his car. Her contoured buttocks draped in the form-fitting designer skirt accentuated her slim, tapered waistline. Once the trunk was closed, after slamming it several times, Martha stood unmoving as if in a trance.

"Where am I going to go?" she asked, perplexed.

Marion scoffed, "Pfft! Anywhere you want, Baby."

Together they drove to the airport Hilton, where he explained the next step before checking her in.

Chapter 4

Monday 8:08 p.m.

Holding his sixth beer, Hank sat at home in his tattered recliner staring at the front door, his index finger tapping the soiled armrest, his right foot twitching nervously.

"That fuckin' bitch," he thought. "That cocksucking whore. She didn't go to work, someone saw her at the bank with some guy, and now she is over an hour late."

He was going to beat her to within an inch of her miserable life when she got home. He visualized grabbing her by her hair and bashing her head against the wall. What was she up to? Did she think he was an idiot? He rehashed the day's events in his head. She took the car, which she never did. That fuckin' ninny never drove farther than the grocery store, but that morning she took the car . . . Why? She was at the bank . . . Why? She couldn't have taken the money, since there wasn't any. They only had a small chequing account so they could maintain cheque-cashing privileges. So what was she up to? Who was that guy Marty saw her with? Was she having an affair? Who the fuck would touch that skank bitch, never took care of herself anyway, not like Jackie, now that's pussy. Downing his last beer he threw the empty can at the door. Let the bitch clean up the mess when she got home. He'd fuck her ass when she'd bend over to clean the litter.

Yeah, Jackie, now that's a piece of ass. He'd track her down tomorrow and give her the fucking she deserves. He'd show her what she missed. Thoughts of Jackie's big tits jiggling beneath him as he fucked the living daylights out of her lulled him to sleep.

Tuesday 9:28 a.m.

Hank groggily reached over and answered the phone with an impatient "HELLO!"

"Mr. Kowalski?" the voice on the line asked.

"Yeah, what?" Hank gruffly answered.

"This is Jack Henderson from Perkins Chemical."

Hank bolted upright from his recliner, in which he had inadvertently spent the night. His hand to his forehead, he nursed a momentary dizzy spell.

"YES . . . yes, sir. How are you, sir?"

"Fine, thank you. You've applied for work at our facility—"

"Yes, yes, I did, a while ago!" Hank stammered.

"Well, a supervisory position has opened up in our shipping department and we're considering you for the position. Would you be interested?"

Hank stood bolt upright at attention. "Yes, yes, absolutely Mr. Henderson, sir!"

"Good, can you be here in an hour?"

"Er, well, my wife has the car."

"Then be here as soon as possible. I'm willing to bend my schedule for a man of your calibre. You know where we are."

"Yes, sir, I'll be there shortly, sir."

Marion, sitting in his car next to Martha, watched the house from down the street as he hung up his cell phone.

"He took the bait," Marion informed her.

Martha could barely contain her combined excitement and amusement; she hugged Marion and planted a firm kiss on his cheek. Marion stepped out of the car and informed the men waiting in the moving truck parked behind them that they would be going in soon.

Hank ran into the shower, shaved, dressed, and left the house in record time. Both Marion and Martha snickered when he came out of the house kicking up beer cans and stumbling when he bolted out the door. Once he'd turned the corner, both he and the movers swung into action.

Martha seemed invigorated as she walked up to the front door with a determined stride. Her Burgundy Ralph Lauren polo top and white slacks gave her an air of confidence. Only her hair and makeup-less face betrayed the old Martha. She inserted her key in the door, unlocked it, and swung it wide open, inviting the movers inside. The four men stormed in, not unlike a strike-force going into action. Martha followed close behind, but once inside she froze. The musty smell of her house triggered a reaction of fear, vulnerability, and discomfort, which immobilized her. She stood paralyzed, and the hint of confidence she had felt till now quickly dissipated.

"Martha, Martha . . . MARTHA!" Marion called.

She spun around, stunned, as if awakened from a deep trance.

"Martha," Marion spoke softly now that he had her attention. "Martha, just the necessities. Remember it's time to lighten your load, not make it heavier."

She nodded in agreement, "We'll start with the upstairs." She bolted up the staircase with the men following close behind.

She pointed out items of interest to her: family heirlooms, pictures, mementos, various pieces of furniture, as one of the men affixed labels on the items to be removed. Marion remained downstairs, looking around him with disdain. He knew of Hank's reputation, moments ago he saw what he looked like, and now he knew how he smelled. Body odour hung heavily in the air. How this woman tolerated this man around her, or worse, in her, he couldn't fathom.

The men started coming down with boxes, pieces of furniture; Marion frowned at some of the items, but maintained protocol and said nothing. In about an hour the undertaking was completed. Just as they were about to leave, he instructed two of the men to take the recliner. Martha looked at him puzzled.

"Why? I don't want it," she said.

Marion explained: "Two reasons: the first to destroy his self-confidence; the second, if ever you have doubts about what we've done, just sit in it and take a whiff."

Martha nodded in agreement at his logic before stepping out. In the car once again, she sobbed uncontrollably. Marion let her be.

Hank walked quickly from the bus stop to the plant's office. The short sprint saved time, but caused him to perspire profusely. His greasy hair slicked back, face carelessly shaven, his cabana shirt soaked in sweat, and polyester pants that no longer fit, he flashed a wide, yellow grin at the repulsed young receptionist.

"I'm here to see Mr. Henderson, Miss."

"Who?" She asked, perplexed.

"Mr. Henderson—he's in personnel, I believe," Hank clarified, still smiling.

"There's no one here by that name, sir," the girl informed him.

The smile vanished from Hank's face. "But I have an appointment."

"Sir, there is no Henderson here," she adamantly stated.

"Just get me Henderson, Missy, I'm late as it is," he ordered.

"Sir, I would, if we *had* a Henderson."

"Then get me your boss, princess. I got no time to waste." Raising his voice.

"Oh, Mr. HENderson!" she said. "I'm sorry. Just a moment, please."

She pressed the P.A. button: "999 main lobby, 999 main lobby." Then, to Hank, "Please have a seat, sir. He'll be here momentarily."

"I thought so . . . Bitch," he muttered under his foul breath.

While he waited, he thought to himself that as soon as he got the job, first thing on his agenda was to get this cunt fired. He didn't have time to think of much else. Two security guards entered the lobby from a side hallway; the receptionist pointed towards Hank, and both men quickly stood before him, shielding the girl. The older of the two said sternly,

"Sir, please leave the property."

"I'm here to see Henderson."

The guard, eyebrows raised, turned to look at the girl.

She responded with a shrug, "I told him. He won't believe me."

"Sir, I've been here eighteen years; there's no Henderson," the guard informed him.

"Fuck you, I've got an appointment!" Hank yelled back.

The men grabbed an arm each and dragged him kicking and scratching all the way to the main gate, where they told him to get lost. Knowing their jurisdiction ended at the property line, he loitered a while, swearing and hurling insults, till finally he ran out of energy and walked away. On the bus ride home he was still despondent and obnoxious, getting thrown off the bus by the driver five blocks from home for annoying other passengers.

The walk served to further piss him off. As he turned the corner of his block, a moving truck was turning the corner down the street. His first thought was that another family of niggers was probably moving in. He walked up to his front door. Stepping into the house, he immediately noticed his recliner was missing. He stood galvanized on the same spot on which Martha had frozen not long before. His eyes took a quick inventory of the living room: TV, stereo, major appliances were all there, but pictures, mementos, kitchen radio were missing. He ran up to the second floor, where the odd item was missing, but other things were untouched.

Thoughts raced through his mind till one stuck: *the whore left me*. He lost it, punching walls, overturning furniture, yelling at the top of his lungs. Then, in a moment of lucidity, it dawned on him . . . the bank!

Marion and Martha led the truck to a cross-town storage complex. There they stored Martha's possessions in a small unit. The movers left after receiving a hundred-dollar tip each for a quick and well-done job. From there, Marion drove Martha back to her hotel, since he was neglecting responsibilities attached to his practice. Martha had rebounded from her emotional breakdown of the morning; as a matter of fact, after leaving the storage plaza she seemed cheerful, and at one point even joked about their exploit.

He had noticed her pleasant smile when she grinned, seeing Hank rushing out of the house, heading for the fictitious interview. Now he saw the true essence of her well-hidden beauty: her laugh was a hearty, exquisitely feminine cackle, which displayed her symmetrically perfect, straight white teeth. Her eyes seemed to light up and glitter when she allowed herself to delight in life. Judging from the lack of laugh lines around her eyes and the presence of frown lines on her forehead, she surely rarely took pleasure in circumstance. She quickly suppressed her pleasant laugh as if embarrassed by it; Marion had to chuckle at her self-consciousness. He believed that her newly acquired riches as well as breaking free of that tyrant would cause her self-esteem to blossom. What had started for him as a financial opportunity seemed to be evolving into an attachment to the shy, vanquished woman.

Marion pulled up to the upscale hotel where she was staying. A valet opened her door, but she sat once again, sad and staring at her feet.

"Must you go, Marion?" she asked pensively.

"Yes, I've got to get back to the office. Tell you what, I'll come back this evening and we'll have supper together. Think you could afford to treat me?" he teased.

She beamed at the idea, "Yes, I'll be looking forward to it." She gave him an excited schoolgirl hug before exiting the car.

Tuesday 11:16 a.m.

Hank stormed out of the house in a blind rage. He didn't even bother changing his shirt, which was now button-less from his scuffle with the bus driver. Quickly he marched down the street towards the local branch of the bank. With demented determination, he stormed through the door and looked around him. His vision focused on Phillips, who was seated at his desk in his office going over some papers with one of the female tellers.

Hank barged through the open office door in a fury. Red-faced, huffing, dishevelled, and perspiring, he stood in front of Phillips's desk. Hank's eyes radiated rage, his fingers clenched in fists that hung at his sides trembling. Phillips wheeled his chair back against the wall while the girl darted past Hank and ran out.

He spat the question, "Why the fuck was she here yesterday?"

Holding his hands up, palms out, Phillips assumed a defensive posture. Staying seated, he asked Hank to calm down. The request made Hank angrier still. He leaned over the desk and in one swoop swept everything on it to the floor.

"Tell me! Now!"

Hank's spittle struck Phillips's face. Phillips stood and cowered in the corner of his office. He could see behind Hank that the business in the bank had ceased; all stopped to stare, some clients left, and one of his tellers was on the phone speaking urgently.

"Hank, please sit down, I'll explain."

As he looked over Hank's shoulder, one of the tellers signalled him by twirling a finger over her head indicating revolving lights. That was their signal that the police had been called. Phillips gave a tiny nod, confirming he understood.

Hank hesitated, considering his offer. Finally he sat, his eyes wide and predatory. Phillips eased back down into his own chair.

"Don't fuckin' lie to me, Phillips. I was told she was here—here with a man! WHAT THE FUCK FOR!" His rage welled up again.

"Yes, yes, she was. Let me tell you the whole story." Phillips spoke slowly and calmly; he knew he had to buy some time.

"Would you like a coffee, Hank?"

"DON'T FUCK WITH ME, PHILLIPS!" Hank roared, slapping the desk with his palms and rising halfway to his feet.

"Okay, okay, Hank, I'll tell you everything . . . She came in to discuss the money from a pool she won at work. She wanted to put it in a bond that would pay better interest than a savings account."

"YEAH? AND WHO THE FUCK WAS THAT GUY SHE WAS WITH?"

Just then Phillips saw two policemen enter the bank, guns drawn, and one of the girls pointed to Phillips's office. Phillips quickly put his hand up indicating all was under control but waved them to come in. The two officers glanced at each other and reluctantly holstered their weapons. Hank spun around in his chair, stood, and looked around, like a trapped animal.

He focused on Phillips, who was still sitting, and hissed, "Motherfucker!"

"Hank, calm down before something bad happens, please," Phillips begged. He then addressed the officers, "This man is distraught. Could you please just escort him out, gently. I don't wish to press charges, I just want him out."

The policemen did as he requested; however, there was nothing gentle about it. One twisted his arm behind his back while the other clasped his collar, pulling him out the front door. Once out in the street, words were exchanged. Hank finally went on his way when they threatened to bring him in on charges. Phillips wiped sweat and spit from his forehead, and once he assured the staff all was well, they returned to work. He took the precaution of calling Mrs. Kowalski's lawyer to inform him of what had just ensued.

Martha sat on the hotel suite's bed. It was early afternoon and she felt restless. She contemplated what to do till Marion came back, as well as how her feelings for him had changed in such a short span of time. Shortly after their initial meeting, she had regarded him with contempt; then mistrust, which quickly evolved to guidance; to relying on him as a crutch; to liking him; and now she felt a full-blown attraction.

Restless, she searched the room for something to read. Opening a drawer in the writing desk, she found the hotel directory. Bringing it to the bed she lay down and started leafing through it. She had butterflies in her stomach, so eating was of no interest. Then she saw the publicity for the hotel's beauty salon:

COIFFURE, MANICURE, WAXING, MASSAGE,
TANNING FACILITIES, AESTHETICIAN

"Hmm," she thought. Rising and going to the dresser mirror, she gave herself a once-over. She was pleased with the new clothes; she had felt out of place in them at first, but it didn't take long for her to warm up to the new look. She pulled her dangling, limp hair up, turning her head from side to side. She hadn't had her hair done properly since her wedding day; visits to the salon were limited to a quick shampoo and a trim. Her eyebrows were bushy by most women's standards; she noted a few errant hairs on her chin and upper lip. Pulling off her polo, she exposed her breasts, noting a few more unflattering hairs around her nipples. She never could allow herself the luxury of making herself attractive, since Hank would insult or hit her if she looked too good, calling her slut, whore, hooker, bitch . . . So she tried to look plain, preferring not to attract attention from him or others. Picking up the phone, she called the number, and they gave her an appointment for an hour hence.

Marion walked into his office to find a patient visitor, whom he immediately recognized as working for Vincent, his bookie. His secretary was typing something. Marion knew that typing profusely was her way of escaping reality. The burly man stood defiantly, exhaling loudly through his nose. He'd been waiting since morning and wasn't a happy camper. Marion bowed his head in greeting and indicated his office using his hand, which held his briefcase.

The man went in, followed by Marion.

"Hold my calls," he told his secretary. Marion stepped behind his desk, inviting the man to sit.

"Mr. Vincent—" the man began, but Marion cut him off.

" Five thousand, I know, I know."

"Seven thousand, now," the man corrected.

"Fine, seven thousand. Listen, tell Vinnie—"

"Mr. Vincent," the man corrected again.

"Okay, tell *Mister* Vincent," Marion repeated, "that he can count on the money. I'm working on a case that's going to be paying off very big, very soon."

"Mr. Vincent told me to not to come back without the money."

Annoyed, Marion picked up the phone and dialed Mr. Vincent's number. Mr. Vincent, a.k.a. Vincenzo Rinaldi, a.k.a. Frenchy, a.k.a. The Gent, finally answered the phone. Marion explained that his man was sitting before him and that he'd like to negotiate a deal. Marion proposed doubling the interest till he paid him, which wouldn't be later than in a couple of weeks. Mr. Vincent contemplated the offer for a moment prior to accepting, but not before reminding him of the physical pain or mortality issues attached to the agreement. Marion passed the phone to Mr. Vincent's goon. After receiving instructions from his boss, the man passed the receiver back to Marion to hang up. He then rose to leave.

"Excuse me, what's your name?" Marion asked.

The man turned and without humour in his voice or face asked, "Why? You wanna date me?"

With a nervous laugh Marion replied to his question, "No, no, I was wondering if you moonlighted, you know, took care of business after hours."

"Maybe, but you'd have to deal with Mr. Vincent for that."

"Thank you, I understand," Marion acknowledged.

After the man left, Marion peered out his office door to see his secretary still profusely typing something or other.

"Okay, we're open for business," he informed her.

She turned and gave him a stack of pink memo sheets with messages, pointing out one that she informed him seemed more urgent than the others:

Dan Phillips
Worker's Bank
555-2755
Extremely urgent!!!

Marion called him back immediately.

Hank walked into his usual hangout, pissed, sore, and thirsty. When his eyes became accustomed to the dim lighting of the bar, he spotted the bartender and Jackie huddled over something on the bar. Jackie turned to see him, and jumped to her unsteady feet, taking a step towards him.

"Oh, lover, what happened to you? Come here, Baby. Were you in a fight?" she inquired, concerned.

He brushed her aside as he headed for the bar.

"Scotch with a beer chaser," he ordered. The bartender sprang to action, but his eyes seemed to be studying Hank. Jackie staggered up to Hank and, putting her arms around his neck, whispered in his ear accusatorily,

"You never said a word even while you were fucking me."

Hank turned his head to look at her with a mixture of irritation and questioning. "What are you talking about? Today's not the day to yank my fuckin' chain."

Astonished at his response, she took a step back, gave him a coy look, and slid the paper she was looking at before him. He looked at the section she pointed out:

LOTTERY RESULTS
OVER 19 MILLION WON THIS WEEK

He panned to the line Jackie indicated with a chipped fake nail: *Martha Kowalski, a local resident, is the winner of $8.6 million in yesterday's draw. No comment as to what she planned to do with her winnings. (Photo unavailable)*

His mouth fell open; he picked up the paper and walked towards the stained glass windows, where the light was a little better. With a frown he read and reread the article. Jackie and the bartender glanced at each other questioningly. Hank snapped. Picking up a chair he flung it through the front window in a rage, uttering a primal yell.

Martha sat in the aesthetician's chair, her face concealed by a mud mask. Two women were working on her at once, one doing her manicure, while the other filed the calluses on her feet with a pumice stone. Martha relished the attention, excited at the thought of what she would look like when all was finished. She received the full treatment: manicure, facial, waxing, massage, and finally a session in the tanning booth before having her hair cut, dyed and styled. She even allowed them to do her bikini line, blushing the entire time.

When it was over several hours later, she beheld herself in the mirror. She was astonished at what she saw—a beautiful, sexy woman. The makeup accentuated her dark eyes. Her hair was a light auburn with blonde highlights and framed her glowing, symmetrically perfect face. The girls proudly called over their colleagues to flaunt their work. Congratulations were uttered all around, and sincere compliments were directed at Martha.

One effeminate hair stylist who was obviously gay commented to everyone's amusement, "My God, this may be the one who could convert me."

She stood and hugged everyone. They cautioned her not to cry, since it would smudge her makeup. Laughing, she thanked them profusely and, after signing the considerable salon bill, returned to her room. Once there, she spent the next long while admiring herself in awe.

Marion spoke with Phillips; he worried regarding the information that he just received. Maybe Hank Kowalski was crazier and more violent than he had assumed. The thought of a restraining order was premature, since Hank didn't know where to find Martha, but using Mr. Vincent's unconventional services would remain an option.

Hank sat in the cell at the municipal police station. He was cut, bruised and bleeding. He sat quietly breathing deeply through his nose. The wave of information and events of the day further disrupted his already disturbed state of mind. From the front he could hear Jackie hysterically arguing with what he assumed was the sergeant in charge, "You had no right to arrest him. He'll pay for the fuckin' window. He's a millionaire, you know!"

Chapter 5

Martha was killing time by trying on her newly acquired wardrobe. She was still incredulous at her transformation within the last couple of days. The bed was strewn with the various skirts, blouses, pants, tops . . . but it was the undergarments that struck her. Her body had been draped in unstylish and inexpensive polyester and simple cotton clothing all her life; she was brought up to be humble and taught to be ashamed of her body.

Living by those standards, she had spent her life with her head in the sand, believing in her man for better or worse. She'd seen the "worse"— when was the "better" going to kick in? Subscribing to those ideals you could never have your hopes crushed, mainly because there was no hope. Martha had followed her mother's guidance and had married the first thing that came along: namely Hank, who had been handpicked by her abusive, alcoholic father. Martha was told that Hank was a good man, since he could hold his liquor. Their courtship had consisted of his going over to her place after his shift at the rendering plant and drinking with her father.

For six months he'd been over every night, barely saying a word to Martha. He'd stop by after supper—at least he'd had the decency to shower and shave then—always the same clothes, same gelled, unkempt hair, same cheap aftershave in a futile attempt to cover up the stench of rotting animal carcasses. He'd give her a peck on the cheek and head straight for the living room to watch TV with her father, sitting on the overstuffed, frayed couch. They'd toast their success at being the superior gender, at being masters of their small, meaningless domain, and at keeping their women reliant on their meagre providence.

Once a week or so, her "boyfriend" would take her for a "drive." She certainly learned quickly what *that* implied. Straight to make-out point, where he would unceremoniously park, undo his belt, unzip his pants, and pull out his ripe, urine-scented cock. With a wink and a yellow-toothed smile, he'd coax her along. At first he'd settle for a hand job, but it was not long before he was insisting on her sucking it.

At sixteen, when Martha told her mother what he'd expect from her on their outings, her mother shrugged it off, saying, without ever lifting her eyes from her sewing, "Sweetheart, that's a thing every man wants. If it'll keep their feet on the ground and their fists in their pockets, then it's a small price to pay."

So Martha fulfilled her responsibilities; she whacked and sucked him off. Allowed him to slobber all over her breasts, finger her pussy. The whole time she struggled to hold back a retch and was glad to have him come in her face, which meant he'd be driving her back home.

Those memories served to strengthen her resolve to now break free from that existence; to live out whatever was left of her life in prosperity and happiness.

She called Marion and he told her he'd clear up some loose ends and then they'd go out for supper. But she had made other plans for them that evening.

Hank made bail with Jackie's help. She came up with the three hundred dollars. She had seventy-five dollars in her bra and the rest under a floorboard in her apartment. Hank recognized her help, but he'd never stoop so low as to thank a mere woman. He figured he'd give her that long overdue fucking she deserved and that would square things away.

The public defender suggested to Hank that an offer to pay for the damages and an apology should get him a suspended sentence even with the charge of resisting arrest. Hank's reply was, "Pay for damages? I'll buy the whole fuckin' place before my court date." Jackie slipped her arm around Hank's. He made no attempt to acknowledge her, which she overlooked, content with stumbling along trying to keep up with her new man's stride.

Once back at his house, Hank paced back and forth nervously where his recliner had been, mumbling to himself incoherently. Jackie tried to comfort him.

"C'mon, Hank, it's for the best. You were too good for the ungrateful bitch. Tomorrow we'll get the money. Let me take care of you." She took a step towards him in an attempt to embrace him.

The moment her hand touched his shoulder, he swung around and struck her. Jackie fell to the floor. He pounced on her as she struggled to get up on her hands and knees. Lifting her short skirt around her waist he ripped her panties off. He undid his belt and let his pants drop around his knees. Kneeling behind her, he stroked his penis in preparation. Jackie begged him to stop, but he was in no mood to take orders from a woman. He struck her repeatedly, aggravated that his manhood wasn't functioning immediately. He finally got it up enough to penetrate her.

He fucked her violently, releasing all his frustrations from the trying day he had had. He took pleasure in seeing the cunt writhe in pain as his cock assaulted her. She dared storm out on him yesterday—now she wasn't going anywhere till he was finished. He humped her while hurling insults at her and all the women of the world. He took pleasure in hearing her whimpering cries. Finally he was achieving satisfaction, ejaculating in her, letting her go only once his flaccid, cum-dripping cock plopped out of her. He left her sobbing on the floor.

Marion let himself in with his room key.

"Martha, you here?"

She answered his call from the suite's bathroom. "Just a minute, I'll be right out."

She had put away all the clothes she had tried on in the afternoon, choosing a dress she felt was suitable for the evening. He noted a small, round table with chairs had been set up in the living-room area.

"Aren't we going out?" he asked.

"No, if you don't mind, we'll eat in . . . I'm not feeling myself tonight."

Marion turned to see her entering the room. She stood in a simple, elegant black dress, which stopped at mid-thigh. His jaw dropped and his eyes widened in a look of absolute astonishment. She was more than pleased with his reaction; she blushed and giggled, even finding the courage to do a twirl. He admired her figure draped in the low-cut backless designer dress. He couldn't help but walk up to her with his arms out. He placed his hands on her hips and held her at arms length admiring her. Trying unsuccessfully to speak, he managed only to gurgle incoherently before getting out the simple statement: "Beautiful . . . My God, you're beautiful!"

A knock came at the door; Marion pulled away to answer it. Two waiters pushed in a cart with various covered platters. The men proceeded to lay out the place settings. With the waiters holding out their chairs, Marion and Martha took their places across from each other at the cozy little table. Once the waiters had served the soup and entrees, and the champagne was chilling in the bucket, Martha tipped them and signed the receipt before they took their leave.

They both had a most pleasant meal; Martha had quite a taste for good food, Marion thought. Martha flushed when he complimented her, but confessed that she didn't know what half the items on the menu were. She admitted to him that she had simply ordered a romantic dinner for two from room service and they took care of the rest. *Romantic, eh?* Marion thought, smiling.

He was still in a state of shock at Martha's transformation. She asked him if he thought it was too much, and he assured her that it was overdue, but certainly not overdone. Conversation began to take on a romantic tone and, with the whirlwind of events over the past couple of days, it dawned on Martha that she knew nothing of Marion Lloyd. Was he married? Divorced? Gay? She asked him to tell her about himself.

Uncorking another wine bottle, he poured them both a glass of fine Bordeaux. He accommodated her by narrating that he'd been a lawyer for the past five years. In an attempt to placate his father, he had gone into law. It was very tough pleasing him, because he was constantly pushing him to the limit. Good was never good enough for his father. Marion then changed the subject, seeming uneasy about relating his life story. Martha would have liked to hear more, but she realized she'd hit a sore spot. She rarely got the opportunity to listen to life experiences that differed from her own, and never had anyone taken the time to discuss something with her. People spoke *of* her or *to* her but never conversed *with* her.

He fast-forwarded to when he'd decided to go it on his own, not having appreciated the constraints imposed by working for a law firm. Things were rough in the beginning, and now it wasn't much better, but he had no regrets—taking the opportunity to mention his debts.

She took the bait, asking how much he owed. With a forlorn expression he told her. Without hesitation she offered to help him, now that she could, as long as he kept helping her deal with her newfound wealth. He humbly but readily accepted her offer. He had had no other interest in her except for profit from her newfound wealth; however, he found her naïveté endearing, and now that he saw her transformation from plain to stunningly beautiful, he wanted more than her money.

Martha was relieved to hear that he was not married or seeing anyone presently. She opened up to him when Marion asked her what had kept her from leaving her husband until now. She began by explaining that she cared little for her wicked father's feelings or opinions. He was strict and abusive, treating her, as well as her mother, like a possession. There had been no love in her home except between her mother and her.

Her father literally always had the upper hand. He beat his wife often, blaming her for everything. Martha saw no other option than to stay with Hank. One reason was that her father thought Hank was the greatest thing since sliced bread; he would certainly disapprove of a breakup. Martha would then expose herself to the wrath of both Hank and her father. She also feared that her mother would pay dearly for her decision as well. Martha's mother wouldn't hear of the possibility of her breakup; she would counsel Martha to be more submissive. She couldn't blame her mother; she, too, had been raised without options. Besides not possessing the means or resources to leave him till now, she feared Hank would seek her out and surely kill her if she did.

Marion changed the subject. The conversation had taken them through dessert, and although it had been interesting as well as therapeutic for them both, it was now regressing to a depressing exposé. Martha's voice had begun to tremble at the thought of her wasted life to date. Reaching over for the champagne bottle, he took Martha by the hand and led her to the couch by the window. He told her that was enough of the past; now they would talk of the future.

Their discussion evolved to discussing matters of the heart, relationships, love, then finally sex. The view of the airport from the large upper-floor bay window was beautiful. The many shimmering lights were mesmerizing. Uncorking the bottle, Martha was startled, giggling at her excitability. He poured each of them a glass, and they made toasts to both their health and happiness.

Marion asked her what her plans were. She replied she had absolutely no idea of what she was going to do with her winnings. The money would provide the means, but her self-confidence would have to be developed. He once again tried to make her fathom what that kind of money could provide for her. She now had a chance to break away from this boring industrial town, move where she wanted to, and as many times as she cared to. Perhaps a cabin up north; an apartment in New York; a getaway home in Florida, Bahamas, Europe? She laughed at the suggestion.

This caused Marion to sit up, and with a serious tone he leaned towards Martha, saying: "Martha, you will have to realize that this is not just a lucky break, this is a major windfall. You have the world by the tail! I'm proud and pleased that you took the initiative to do what you did today. This morning you showed courage in taking back what was yours; this afternoon you showed spirit and confidence in changing your appearance. It demonstrates a will, ambition, and I'm proud of you. Promise me that you'll master your life, that you'll take the bull by the horns and pursue your dreams."

"Yes," she declared, leaning forward and kissing Marion on the mouth.

Marion was surprised at her bold move; he accepted her advance willingly. They kissed tentatively at first. Marion attempted to deep kiss her, but was met by a closed mouth from her.

Martha unconsciously had wanted this moment since Marion had left for work earlier that day. Left by herself, the empty feeling of unfulfilled love haunted her thoughts. The empty, luxurious hotel room containing the king-sized bed evoked thoughts of wonder at what had transpired in this room. Sex had to be more than insertion and ejaculation. She had always thought that some of the conversations from the other waitresses at work were a sham, particularly from one who was quite promiscuous.

This coworker would often agree to meet patrons after her shift. The other girls would grill her about what had transpired the night before. She would accommodate them by leaving out no detail. From where they went, to what they did, to how many times they did it. The size of his member, the dexterity of his tongue and how many times and how strong she came.

Martha never understood the meaning of the terms cumming, climax, or orgasm. She knew how it applied to a man, but couldn't fathom its relationship to a woman. Her sexual experience had been pretty much one-sided. Either Hank was not able to get it up, which inevitably translated into verbal abuse directed at her for being ugly and stupid; or he would have a premature ejaculation, which always suited Martha fine. On extremely rare occasions a feeling—no, rather a sensation—started to well up in her, which she didn't comprehend. In her youth it was more present in the beginning of her relationship with Hank. She'd soon realize what that sensation had a potential of blossoming into if nurtured properly.

Marion kissed her lips, face and neck. For a reason he didn't comprehend she didn't allow him to fully embrace her mouth. Marion held her, running his hands up and down her back. He discerned tension in her, and although she had made the first move, she seemed reluctant to fully participate in the lovemaking. He pursued his exploration of the new and improved Martha. He ventured to her breasts, cupping and fondling them through the expensive fabric of her dress. She offered no resistance when he slipped the straps of her garment off her shoulders. He kissed her neck, slowly working his way to her breasts. She was silent—too silent— no evidence of the telltale signs of arousal such as increased breathing or writhing; however, he could feel her heart racing uncontrollably when he slipped his hand inside her bra.

She felt tense; she had often been taken but never induced into giving. As wonderful as it felt to have him touching her, she felt she was being led down a beautiful, yet unfamiliar, path. She allowed him to lead, finally deciding to give her full cooperation. His hands cupped her breasts, he unclasped her bra, she detected a note of admiration on his face before he bowed his head to suckle and kiss them. This tenderness was foreign to her.

She relinquished herself fully to him and gave him complete access; she relished his hands exploring her body. She'd never been touched like this; she'd never been touched lovingly. He eased her atop him, her clothing now shed, she allowed him to spread her as she sat atop his lap. She tentatively nuzzled his neck and face; his clean, scented skin was alien to her. Martha began to express her arousal; she began to feel his manhood harden within his pants. Trained as she had been she dropped to her knees to release his penis. She proceeded to dutifully unzip him but he stopped her.

He took her trembling hand, the one that had started pulling his zipper down. Standing, he helped her to her feet. She stood before him naked except for her lace panties. He saw her embarrassment as he admired her exquisite body. He noticed her looking away self-consciously. He led her to the bed, where he lay her down; there he peeled off his clothes except for his boxers before joining her. Lying next to her, looking deeply into her eyes, he detected a flurry of emotions in her gaze ranging from passion to excitement to lust to wonder and fear. He intended to satisfy all except the last. From there he relished her body, he teased, kissed and stroked her gently and slowly. Finally he arrived at his intended objective. Gently he peeled her panties off, and she discreetly raised her buttocks off the bed for him.

She observed his actions, not yet fully confident to allow herself to be a full-fledged participant. She delighted in his gentle touch; however, she restrained herself from showing her pleasure, preferring to lie stoically, still unsure of herself. She had allowed him to remove her panties more from a mechanical response than willingness. Once her undergarment was removed, she was shocked at his next act. She watched in astonishment as he applied his mouth to her vagina. She had certainly heard of the act, wondered about it, but dismissed it as mere flight of fancy. Her husband had never performed the deed on her; his forte was strictly insertion.

She reluctantly allowed him access to her womanhood, even though she felt uncomfortable about the act. She was forcing herself to allow him to continue. Her reluctance was short-lived, however, as his tongue explored her. Although she had heard of the act that was now being performed on her, she always thought it too unnatural to be true. However, regardless of how unnatural it seemed to her, it was far too pleasing to stop. Arousal was rising past feelings of frustration for the first time in her life.

Arousal always used to leave her unsatisfied; she saw no useful function to it, a futile feeling, depriving her of sleep and diligence. Now she felt for the first time that it would lead to something. She passed for the first time that plateau she had reached on only on a couple of occasions with Hank, only to turn back down that steep hill unfulfilled and empty. She saw that shrouded in mist there was a peak that eluded her. Marion's urging tongue guided her forward, she stumbled a few times on her climb up but he helped her regain her footing. Encouraging her to pursue their trek, not rushing her, but leading her upward by his persistence. As suddenly as she had begun her climb, she was reaching the summit, and she didn't know what to expect once she arrived; however, nature took over and ran its course.

She found herself gasping for air as if she had run a marathon, making sounds she had never before dared make, not realizing that she had pulled the bed linen off the mattress by grasping them so tightly. Then it hit—her first orgasm. She had heard of them, but the concept was unknown to her. She hadn't climbed to the summit; instead, she had burst to the top at incredible speed. Ecstasy and fear were intertwined as Martha stared with eyes wide open at the ceiling during this profound new sensation.

Without realizing it, Martha tightly grasped Marion's head, squeezing it firmly between her quivering thighs with both her hands and legs, crouching forward, wailing her pleasure loudly as though she was truly alone on a mountaintop. Marion stayed with her as she thrashed about like a woman possessed. She leaped from summit to summit, and finally sprawled out on the bed, spent. Marion was red-faced and panting, obviously exhausted from her marathon climax.

Marion kneeled between Martha's open legs, pulling his penis over the elastic band of his underwear. His appendage looked huge and threatening as he guided it towards her waiting vagina. Martha looked at him with tears in her eyes, and he asked, "Are you all right?"

She responded by embracing him deeply as he gently entered her. She soon granted him free rein to her by wrapping her legs around his firm buttocks. He began rocking back and forth. She couldn't help but compare the sensation to that experienced with Hank. Although Marion's organ was average in size, he was considerably larger than Hank. She found the feeling of being filled completely overwhelming. Martha left behind the beaten woman that had endured years of abuse.

Marion's moment was yet to come. She expected him, like Hank, to finish in short order, but he continued to perform. She welcomed his unselfishness and stamina, and soon another peak came into view for her. Martha was being propelled to the top on wings of air. Marion's breathing quickened at the same pace as his thrusts. They reached the top at the same time. She was experiencing another orgasm before he pulled out. He collapsed next to her after his own. Martha, invigorated by the experience, kissed him passionately.

Marion fell asleep shortly after their sexual liaison, his arm around Martha's shoulders. Martha, however, was unable to sleep after her overwhelming experience; she lay awake with her head resting on her lover's chest. She could clearly hear Marion's heartbeat; she took solace and security from him. She now was in love with this man, the only man who had ever recognized her as a person worthy of respect, instead of a worthless possession.

Chapter 6

Martha awoke, startled from her disturbed sleep; the disquieting dream was a recollection of her father's sudden death. Maybe the nightmare was some sort of payback for the pleasure she had experienced only hours before. Marion lay undisturbed by her sudden awakening.

The call she received from her panicked, grief-stricken mother that fateful night still haunted her. It was, oddly enough, about three in the morning—the same as it was now—on a cold, rainy February night. She hadn't heard the phone ring; it was Hank, swearing about who the fuck was calling at this time, that had woken her. He yelled for her to get the phone, even though it was within easy reach for him, just beside where he had fallen asleep on his recliner. She staggered out of bed and ran to answer it, not knowing how many times it had rung when she picked it up.

Sobbing, her mother informed her, "Your father's dead!"

Calmly, "I'll be right over, Mom," was all she said before she set the receiver down.

She told Hank, whose only comment was, "Dead, eh?" before turning on his side and going back to sleep.

Martha dressed and stepped out into the cold, rainy night. She walked the six blocks from her dingy third-floor apartment to her parents' house. Martha stepped in to find her mother sitting in the living room in a state of shock. Martha attempted to comfort her, but her mother wasn't responsive. Finally she asked where her father was, and her mother informed her that he was in the bedroom.

Martha looked up the stairs that led up to the second floor where the bedrooms were. Swallowing hard, she reluctantly climbed up. At the top of the stairs, she looked down the hall and could see her father's blanket-covered feet; as she approached slowly, the body came into view. He lay there in a semblance of sleep, except for his mouth being wide open in a silent cry. She remained in the doorway for just a moment, not wishing or caring to approach.

Once back downstairs, she sat across from her mother, who was still in a hypnotic state staring into space. Finally she managed to recount the events to Martha. She explained that she had awakened to go to the washroom, and halfway down the hall she noted the absence of snoring. She turned back to make sure all was well, but was shocked to find him not breathing. The first thing she did was to call her only daughter.

Once Martha determined that they were the only ones aware of his death, she called an ambulance, which then dispatched the coroner, who then sent them to a funeral home to make arrangements. It was late morning when the body was finally removed. Hank showed up after the body had been transported. His first comment was in relation to her missing work, and that she'd best leave, promising he'd stay. Martha wished to stay with her mother; however, she knew better than to contradict him.

It was a pitifully attended funeral; barely twelve people were at the service. Her father was not a sociable sort, a classic narcissist much like Hank. The service was held very early in the morning. Hank wanted it that way so Martha needn't miss too much work. Martha had been surprised at how much her father's death seemed to devastate her mother. Her mother continued to be uncommunicative and often cried spontaneously, unlike Martha, who remained stoic throughout the entire affair. Martha went to her mother that night after her shift; her mother's demeanour during the funeral had confused her. She knew she hated the man with a passion, yet she seemed to grieve his death wholeheartedly.

Her mother finally confided in her, explaining why. Her father, as she already knew, was abusive towards her mother. He also carried no life insurance. Although he had group insurance coverage at work, he never contributed to the life insurance coverage. Apparently he had told his wife he'd be damned if he'd have seven dollars a week deducted so she could profit from his demise. He was true to his word. He left her with nothing but the mortgaged house, which she couldn't afford to keep, and a savings account of twenty-five hundred dollars after the funeral costs. That amount was just enough to carry her over to her own death four months later. The bank account contained thirty-seven dollars when she passed away. That's why she was crying so hard—not because he was gone, but because he had left nothing behind. Martha realized her mother couldn't afford the luxury of living.

Hank and Martha moved into her parents' house soon after their deaths. Martha picked up a second job in order to afford the mortgage on her inheritance, ownership of which she naively transferred to her father-in-law.

She wiped a tear that fell to Marion's chest before sleep finally overtook her once again.

Wednesday 8:14 a.m.

Hank left the house early that morning with Jackie in tow. She wore large sunglasses and even heavier than usual makeup in order to camouflage her black eye and bruised cheek. Struggling to keep up with Hank's rapid, impatient stride, she found herself often subjected to tirades of her being fat and slow. They had arrived at the office of the lawyer referred to him by his friend Bill Duncan. Bill's wife cleaned him out when they divorced, but Bill claimed he'd have lost a lot more if it hadn't been for this guy. Hank was relieved to see that Richard Murray was a burly, elderly gentleman; he was afraid it might be one of these young smartasses who thought they knew it all.

Richard Murray disliked Hank the second he met him. Hank's wife truly was an idiot—as he described her—if she had waited this long to leave him. Then again, if he'd let his scruples guide him, he'd have been bankrupt by now. Richard listened to Hank badmouth his wife, calling her every unsavoury name in the book, till he patiently asked him why exactly he was here. Hank then went straight to the point. Richard sat with eyebrows raised at the surprising events that Hank recounted. Hank had brought along the newspaper article as proof. Jackie wordlessly nodded in agreement at Hank's every word.

Richard weighed the facts he had been presented. He then explained to Hank that, based on the information related to him, yes, he would be entitled to a chunk of the winnings, if not half, whether or not he and Martha remained together. Jackie frowned at the thought of Hank's taking his wife back; but was gratified to hear that her cleaning him out and leaving would be construed as malicious and illegal.

Hank sat back in his seat, satisfied with what he heard, clasping his hands behind his head and exposing large damp spots of perspiration under his arms. His face displayed a big, yellow, victorious grin. Richard tempered his enthusiasm by explaining to him that before moving forward, first she'd have to be found.

"If you feel you can track her down, fine; if not, you'd be wise to hire a detective, Mr. Kowalski." He then inquired, "I don't suppose there was any abuse in your marriage directed at your wife."

"Not any more than necessary," Hank replied with his sickening grin. Jackie nodded in agreement.

They both left to meet with the detective that Mr. Murray recommended. Detective Bill Wincott was also to Hank's liking as well: he was in his early sixties, overweight, and chomping on a thick cigar. He, too, listened intently to Hank's account and was willing and able to take on the case. He needed to start immediately, since Martha had already picked up her winnings and now had the means to disappear very quickly. He asked where, when, and who last saw her. Hank revealed that the bank manager was the last to see her, but he wouldn't talk about it. Richard questioned Hank, who insisted impatiently that that was all he knew; but with the detective's persistence Hank unwittingly revealed far more information than he thought.

Marion woke to a most pleasant treat that morning. He looked down to find Martha generously stroking and sucking his penis. She obviously wished to please him, so he allowed himself the luxury of not interrupting her. When he felt his arousal close, he pulled her up and sat her atop him, entering her.

Martha appreciated his desire for her; she felt more confident than the night before. She received him gladly. Till then she had experienced only two sexual positions: missionary and on all fours—Hank would never allow a mere woman to have the controlling position in any situation. They made love, and she again experienced multiple orgasms. She had rapidly gained a genuine appreciation for them, cherishing every one like a lost treasure. She gained a new level of hatred for Hank, for depriving her of this pleasure for so many years.

Marion was surprised that she had initiated sex the way she had. The night before, she had given the impression of a deer caught in headlights; mechanical in her lovemaking, almost like a virgin afraid of what was in store for her, she had given the impression of not wanting to be lost in the moment, but to remain alert and prepared for any eventuality. This morning, however, she was more relaxed, and even closed her eyes. They enjoyed one another fully, much more in tune than during the tentative sex of the night before. Once both were satisfied, they ordered breakfast.

Marion was running late. As much as he wanted to spend the day with her to explore and re-explore every inch of her body and mind, he did have a ton of unfinished business, calls to return, and two court hearings that day. On his way out of the shower, he grabbed a slice of buttered toast off the breakfast tray; then, dressed, he kissed Martha on the cheek before heading out the door. Before leaving, he promised to be back in the afternoon so they could get her debit and credit cards at the bank.

Hank's drinking buddy Marty was at the bank when Martha and her mystery man went to deposit their winnings. And they could trace the origin of the call that sent Hank on a wild goose chase to Perkin's Chemicals, as well the moving truck he had seen turning the corner of his street. He had recalled its conspicuous lime-green colour, which led them to a local moving company by the name of Trans City Movers. To the ordinary person the information was negligible; however, to a seasoned hound dog like Bill Wincott, what little they had was worth gold.

Bill gave Hank and Jackie a lift to Hank's father's house before going to speak to Marty Fitz.

Hank and Jackie rapped on the screen door of his father's house. A thin, older man opened the door partially. He held his fifty-seven years well. Even when he saw his son at the door, he still inquired what he wanted before offering to let him in.

"What is it?" he demanded in a gruff voice while eyeing Jackie suspiciously.

"Pop, I need to talk to you, it's important."

The old man didn't respond except to turn and walk back into the house, leaving the door ajar. When Hank and Jackie walked in, they found him sitting at the modest kitchen table reading the paper and drinking coffee. His head was down as he scrutinized an article; his reading glasses were perched on his nose.

"Pop, I need your help."

"What else is new?" the old man commented sarcastically.

"Martha left me."

"Really? 'Cause of this star, I suppose," thumbing in Jackie's direction without looking up.

"No, no, let me explain. She won, er, some money with the provincial lottery," Hank continued.

The old man finally looked up from his newspaper at his son who stood across from him.

"She took the money and disappeared, and I had to hire a lawyer and a detective to track her down. I could use your help in paying them till they track her down."

The old man stared at his son, removing his glasses; then, crossing his arms while leaning back in his chair, he finally offered his full attention. His son fidgeted nervously. Hank outweighed his father by a good fifty pounds, yet still he felt small next to him—frightened, even.

"How much money did she win, son?" he calmly inquired with a nervous twitch.

Hank looked away and down when he divulged the number. "Around . . . eight million dollars, Pop."

The father didn't even flinch; he calmly took one more sip of coffee and put his cup down.

"Eight million . . . eight million dollars . . . eight fuckin' million!" He stood, launching into a tirade, "Eight motherfuckin' million dollars, you big fuckin' idiot." Mr. Kowalski took small steps toward his son as he continued. "And on top of that, she left you? Why? 'Cause of this cocksucking whore? You fuckin' idiot. Never could keep your head on straight. Never had the brains!"

With that he took a swing at his son, striking him dead center to the side of his head with his closed fist. Hank lurched after being hit. His father immediately directed his anger at Jackie.

"Get the fuck outta here, I've got business with my boy!"

Jackie didn't question or argue. She immediately stood up, turned around, and ran out the door. She looked back just before exiting the house to see the old man pinning Hank to the wall and thrusting his face to Hank's. Hank's lower lip quivered in fear even though he was a good eight inches taller than his father. Jackie stopped once she got off the porch, and, from where she stood, had no problems hearing the altercation.

From the sounds of it, Hank was being mercilessly beaten by his father and it was only until he begged like a little child for him to stop that he let up. Once the old man finally finished venting, he gave Hank a chance to speak.

Sobbing, Hank continued, "Pop, please listen. I'm on top of things, the lawyer says even if she leaves me I can still get half, so I got a detective to track her down, what I need is a cash advance to pay them."

"Cash advance, eh kid? What's in it for me?"

"Pop, I'll turn half my house over to you when it's over."

"Half your house? I already own the whole fuckin' thing, remember? Jerk. You owe me that much, or else you would have lost that, too. You fuckin' idiot."

"Okay, okay, half a million, then," Hank countered.

The old man smiled a wicked, heartless sneer. "Half? HALF a million? No . . . I back you up on this, you give me half of what you pull in."

"But Pop—"

"But what? You'd rather that whore outside gets it? You always reasoned with your cock!" Leaning in close, he added with a menacing undertone, "Listen to me, Sonny, you fuck this up, you pay me back every fuckin' penny, I don't give a shit if you pimp that cunt outside to get it or suck cock yourself, but you'll pay me back . . . Understand?"

Hank conceded to turn over half of his take to his father or debase himself trying. He left the house with a cheque covering the lawyer and detective's startup fees. Jackie followed Hank sheepishly, knowing better than to question him on what had transpired.

Bill found Marty Fitz fairly pickled, even though it wasn't yet noon. Marty gave him a description of the man, but couldn't tell him much more than that, except he had a girl's name, but couldn't recall what it was.

Next he went to the phone company's offices, and through a contact got the phone records of calls to Hank's house for the past week. There he pinpointed the call that had misled Hank into leaving the house. He called the number and got a recorded message: "You have reached Marion Lloyd, attorney at law, please leave your name and number and I'll return your call promptly . . . BEEEEP!"

Bill hung up, leaving no message; however, he smiled to himself, "Marion—a man with a girl's name, all right."

Bill retrieved information on, as well as the address of, the lawyer in question. He then proceeded to Trans City Movers. There he met a hard-nosed dispatcher who in no uncertain terms told him to take a hike when he requested the information. Bill explained to him that he was investigating a burglary, and if he'd rather he and his men be charged as accessories to theft, then that was fine by him. The dispatcher reluctantly gave him what he needed. The person who hired them was a man by the name of Marion Lloyd and he paid cash. The pickup was at 128 Pine Street and it was then delivered to Mercantile Storage Plaza on Industrial drive.

Bill Wincott had a very productive day. In a matter of a few hours he'd identified the mystery man, located the missing goods, and was certain to be only a couple of steps behind Martha Kowalski. The trail however ended at the storage plaza. There, the attendant said a woman by the name of Martha Kowalski rented a 150-square-foot unit and paid cash for a year, up front.

Bill then went to Lloyd's office where he staked out his building. Through the DMV he discovered that Marion Lloyd drove a black '92 Volkswagen Jetta with plate number LTN 884. He parked across the street from his building and with a paper and a super-sized coffee settled in for a possible long wait. His only mistake that day was dropping by the bank and soliciting information from Phillips, the manager, to no avail. He felt that was a waste of time, but wasn't all that concerned about Phillips' alerting his quarry.

Marion drove to his office, where he in fact had to clear a backlog of work before putting in more time on Martha's needs. He was again handed a stack of messages, with the one on top once again announcing an urgent message from Mr. Phillips at the bank. "What now?" Marion thought.

When he returned Phillips's call, the manager informed him that a private detective had come by, requesting information on Martha Kowalski. He explained that he had told him nothing and had called Marion immediately. When Marion hung up he felt flushed; obviously someone was trying to track down Martha. Maybe he underestimated Hank Kowalski. He went to the window and scrutinized the street. There he spotted a man patiently waiting in a nondescript burgundy Chevy Impala. Marion would give him an hour in the hope he was waiting for someone else. If he was still there later, he'd have to evade him.

Martha was still in her robe; she felt ill at ease sitting and waiting. After Marion left she leisurely ate breakfast and showered. Now she sat staring blankly at the television screen, thinking. Her sexual experience from the night before had left her wondering. She'd never doubted that Hank was a terrible lover; she knew there was more to sex than what she had experienced all her life with him. The thought lingered in her mind: Was Marion as good as there was, or was it naive on her part to believe so? Marion also appeared extremely aroused by her. Just the fact of seeing a man so engrossed by her boosted her self-confidence enormously. She thought of their involvement, wishing he were there, wishing to touch and be touched again. She bashfully contemplated a quickie, should he get back earlier.

Marion had to leave for his client's court appearance; however, the suspicious car was still parked near the corner in full view of his car. Momentarily he visualized losing him, but logic won over and he decided on a much better alternative. Leaving the building unnoticed via a back door, he exited into the back alley; from there he walked down the service alley, and arrived at the boulevard running alongside his building. There he managed to hail a cab and was quickly on his way. He was grateful for Phillips's call; without it he would have been tailed and eventually would have inadvertently led them to Martha's location. Once at the courthouse, he couldn't shake the thought of the situation closing in on him. He ran into Phil Benjamin on his way to a court appearance.

Phil was a bright young lawyer who had great aspirations. He had graduated from law school recently with top honours, but although he was a great student, in the real world he had zero experience. Nobody will throw you a bone, and landing a case that will put you on the map is a challenge. Phil wanted the fame and fortune *now*. In certain situations this would be considered admirable, but he was starting to get branded as greedy. So although extremely determined, he was considered maybe too ambitious. Marion knew Phil was always open to new opportunities and would be approachable. Many of the others needed more cases or clients like a hole in the head.

Marion approached him with an offer. Without divulging too much, he informed Phil that due to personal reasons he didn't want to get into right now, he had to lighten his caseload. Marion offered him an opportunity to pick up his clients, which would allow Phil to widen his modest client base. Phil enthusiastically accepted the offer; however, his enthusiasm waned when Marion told him that the switch had to be done that day, actually that minute. Phil suddenly felt it was a bit too much too soon.

Still, when Marion turned to leave, Phil chased after him. Marion pulled him into one of the courthouse's many meeting rooms where lawyers and clients met to discuss cases.

Sliding a few files across the table, Marion spent the next hour putting Phil up to speed. Phil frantically took notes as Marion recounted circumstances, situations, and prospects for the cases he had to work on that day. After that was done, Marion exited the courthouse and hailed a cab. The taxi navigated the city streets on its way to the Airport Hilton. Marion had his arm draped on the back of the car's back seat, scrutinizing the traffic behind them. A couple of times he instructed the driver to take a detour or drive around a block a couple of times in order to further reassure himself that he wasn't being tailed.

The elderly driver did as he was asked unquestioningly, probably having had similar requests in the past. Marion spotted him often looking at him in the rearview mirror warily. Once Marion was confident they weren't being followed, he instructed the driver to head for their destination.

He called Martha. She answered cautiously, but her voice quickly lightened up when she heard who it was. He told her he'd be arriving within ten minutes and to meet him downstairs. He was in a white cab and she was to join him; he'd explain the situation then. She tried to press him for more information, but all he would say was to bring everything she had from the bank and nothing else, and to buy dark sunglasses at the hotel boutique before joining him.

She did as he asked, quickly dressing in a sharp-looking gray jumpsuit with a pastel yellow long-sleeved blouse. Quickly she gathered her things and made her way down to the lobby. She was disappointed that they needed to rush; she had spent the day fantasizing about a repeat performance of the night before. She hoped whatever the hurry was that they could take care of it quickly so they would have some quality time together. Once down in the lobby, she had the odd feeling of being observed, men's heads turned, women stared. Feeling exposed, paranoia quickly kicked in.

She still lacked the self-confidence to distinguish that the stares were of admiration or envy; with the men, tinged with lust and the women, jealousy. At a boutique adjacent to the lobby she chose a pair of oval Ray-Bans and picked up a Gucci tote bag for her belongings. She didn't even flinch at the total of over three hundred dollars. She dug into her brown envelope and handed the cashier four one hundreds. With her change in hand, she slipped on her new shades and rushed to the main entrance. Once there, she anxiously waited for Marion.

Marion called Phillips at the bank from the cab, instructing him to make sure all was arranged with the branch situated near the airport. He wanted credit and debit cards in Martha's name, as well as full access to her funds. He received confirmation just as the taxi rounded the corner to the hotel.

Wednesday 1:11 p.m.

Bill Wincott sat in his car. Marion Lloyd's vehicle was still parked outside the building, but he had a bad feeling that he had dropped the ball. Eyeing the scene suspiciously, he decided to check out his hunch. He called Lloyd's office on his cellular, and after three rings a woman answered,

"Marion Lloyd attorney at law."

"Mr. Lloyd, please," said Wincott.

"He's not here right now; may I take a message?" she responded.

"Oh! I was driving by and saw his car out front, I was sure he was in," Wincott declared.

"No, sir, he stepped out this morning for the courthouse."

"Do you know when he'll be back?"

"As far as I know, he'll be gone on business for couple of days, sir."

"Thank you, Miss." He hung up. "Fuck!" he declared before throwing the car in gear and heading for the courthouse.

It was early afternoon. Hank and Jackie were back at the house, and it had been a rough day. He had deposited his father's cheque at a bank other than the one from which he had been ejected. He and Jackie tried to have a drink at his regular hangout, but when the owner saw them walk in, he immediately evicted them. Hank swore and spat at the bartender. Before leaving, he threw a few bills on the sidewalk declaring he could afford to pay for the fuckin' window and that they would beg for his return one day. He stormed away with his head held high, with Jackie close behind giving the proprietor the finger.

Hank had a roll of bills in his pocket, and never having had that much cash at one time he couldn't resist spending some of it. They had loaded up with booze from the liquor store, ordered Chinese food, and picked up some smokes. Now, back at the house, they sat on the couch drinking, eating, and smoking up a storm. Hank sat sprawled on the couch drinking beer, and ordered her to strip for him. She obliged, dancing to the music that blared from the old stereo eight-track. He hurled indignities at her as she twirled, bent, and crouched before him attempting to follow the beat in her inebriated state.

Her hefty breasts swayed to the music. Jackie knew her duties and dropped to her knees in order to satisfy her man. Pulling, sucking, and stroking, she managed to get a partial erection out of him but every time she attempted to mount him it would wane. Naturally Hank blamed his inability to perform on her, slapping and flinging her to the floor. Fortunately for her, when he rose to kick her he snagged his foot on the tattered carpet that covered the floor and fell, striking his head on the coffee table.

Wincott arrived at the courthouse in a huff. He was angry more at himself than at anything or anyone else. Losing a tail happens to everyone, but it's more of an insult when a veteran gets duped so easily. He searched the courthouse for Lloyd till he was directed to Phil Benjamin. He reluctantly approached the young man, and giving him a false name, informed him that it was crucial he get in touch with Marion Lloyd. Phil explained that he was taking on his caseload for an undetermined length of time. Wincott tried to convince the man that he had urgent personal business with Lloyd and it was crucial that he contact him without delay, but Benjamin didn't bite. Wincott called Lloyd's cellular as a last resort.

Marion explained to Martha what was happening. Her newfound self-confidence quickly evaporated at the thought of Hank closing in on her. She suddenly felt vulnerable and exposed. Guilt crept in like a river of slime, but brought with it memories of the abuse, both physical and psychological. Marion was quick to take her into his arms to comfort her. He reassured her that all would be okay. His phone rang; he hesitated to answer it, since it displayed private name and number. On the fifth ring, just before it would have gone to the voice mail, he answered.

"Hello?"

"Mr. Lloyd, this is Frank Yeomans from the bank. I was given your number by Mr. Phillips from our branch." Wincott held his breath at the other end—he wasn't fully confident of his ploy.

"Yes, go on," Marion urged.

"Um, I'm calling regarding Martha Kowalski's account. We have some papers she would need to sign. Can we meet somewhere and sort it all out together?" Wincott continued.

"Well we're on our way to your head office now. Is it regarding the funds transfer?" He asked. Marion had barely finished the sentence before regretting it.

"Oh, um, yes, yes, as a matter of fact it is. I was unaware you were coming," Wincott backtracked.

"Yes, we're meeting with Jack Rollands in twenty minutes," Marion informed him. There was no Jack Rollands; he had cooked up the name to test the caller.

"Of course, yes, I'll give the papers to Mr. Rollands for signature," Wincott said.

"You do that." Marion hung up and instructed the driver to head back to the hotel. Martha looked at him, puzzled.

"They're closing in," he informed her, putting his arm around her shoulders.

Once back at the hotel, Marion called Phillips. He didn't want to, but figured if there was one person he could even remotely trust it would be Phillips. He explained that someone was looking for them and that they had to modify their plan of going to their appointment at his bank's head office. He then gave specific instructions.

Wincott headed for the bank's head office, his confidence renewed. He was now back in the chase! Once at the bank's offices, which were nearby, he drove into the building's underground garage; once parked, he rushed up to the lobby to scout for their arrival. Above ground, he called Murray the lawyer in order to secure a court order to freeze Martha's assets till a court could rule on the legalities of the lottery win. After that he waited, and waited . . . and waited.

Wednesday, 3:23 p.m.

Marion explained to Martha the next necessary course of action. There were two possible options. The first was to bite the bullet and face Hank in court, divorce him, maybe even get a restraining order against him. She could then rebuild her life, move wherever she wanted, do whatever she wanted, and never look back or need to look over her shoulder. However, the cost of following that route was handing over half her winnings to him. The second option was to grab the money and disappear from the face of the earth.

Without hesitation Martha chose the disappearing option. Marion, once convinced of her resolve, called Phillips back to put the plan into action. Martha left Marion to structure the getaway plan. She went into the washroom and decided to take a shower to calm down. Before turning on the shower water, she paused to look at the other corner of the large bathroom where a Jacuzzi sat on an elevated step. Stepping out of the shower, she went over to the tub, where a plaque with instructions sat on the edge. She cocked her head to read,

Activate jets only once tub filled to the waterline
Timer controlled

She proceeded to fill the tub. She couldn't recall the last time she had soaked in a tub. The one she had at home was an old cast-iron job on feet, rust stained and cramped to the point of never considering lying in it; a plastic shower curtain, lacking a few shower rings, surrounded it. Showers had always been a necessity rather than a luxury. Within five minutes, she'd be soaped, rinsed, and dried. She couldn't recall when or if she had ever just soaked a while. When the tub was halfway full, she poured in a small bottle of complimentary bubble bath.

Staring at the building suds generated by the running tap, she ran her hand through the luxurious foam, feeling the soft, warm bubbles. She smiled, anticipating a good soak among their company. Once the tub was filled she pressed the plastic "ON" button situated next to the tap. With a start she watched the tub groan to life, swirling the water about, generating even more lather. Carefully she stepped into the inviting waters, her feet and calves teased by the swirling water. Gently she lowered herself in, giggling as her buttocks and pubis received the pleasurable sensation. Once seated, she lay back with a sigh, her breasts lapped by the welcoming warm water. Within minutes she slipped into an inviting snooze.

She dreamt she was spread out naked beneath a hot sun and gentle waves lapped at her naked body. Although she'd never been to a beach or even seen the ocean, she imagined it was like this. Relishing in the pleasant sensation, she hardly noticed Marion joining her.

She lay spread out beneath the waters, with Marion opposite her in the large Jacuzzi. He slipped his foot between her open legs. Martha acknowledged the sensation with a smile and sighed with content. He lay back with his arms draped over the sides and massaged her mound with his foot. She sank lower into the water giving him better access, her lower lip lapped by the bubbling water. Her eyes remained closed, not wishing to distract her sense of touch with that of sight. Her pelvis was grinding against his toes. Once again she started experiencing the new sensation she had discovered the night before.

Marion looked at Martha opposite of him. He still had trouble believing this was the same meek, unattractive woman that had walked into his office a few days ago. Being a betting man, he would have favoured the odds heavily against him getting involved with her in any way. Had someone bet he'd be at some point sitting in a Jacuzzi with his foot massaging her crotch and glad to be doing it, he'd have discounted him as crazy. Yet here he was, and while she lay back revelling in his attentions, he sat admiring her beauty.

She was close to climax, her back arched, her nipples being exposed to the cool air hardened. Her moans became gasps with her growing arousal. The hard ceramic tiled walls reverberated with her wail when she climaxed. The water cascaded over the rim, propelled by her convulsive movements. He slipped his hand down onto his lap in order to check his readiness, confirming his arousal.

Once her ecstasy subsided, Martha slid over to Marion and straddled him. She wormed and wiggled in his lap till he was finally in her. She then rode him to glory. The bathroom resonated with the sounds of copulation. Moans, gasps, and cries filled and echoed within the enclosed space. Water splashed about and spilled onto the floor. After years of getting badly fucked she was the one taking charge, permitting herself the luxury of uncorking her bottled-up emotions and setting them free. She looked down at Marion's expression of extreme pleasure.

Only a few days ago she looked at him across his cluttered desk with disdain, a man who preferred to belittle rather than help her—just another man who pitied her and maybe even was repulsed by her. Now he was at her mercy! She humped him relentlessly; oblivious to the watery mess they were producing around them. She rode him hard, feeling his member throb within her till he also achieved a welcome orgasm. She lay atop him and they embraced one another till a member of the hotel staff rapped at the door, reporting that water was leaking into the room beneath them.

Chapter 7

The Hilton was just getting over its weekday morning hustle and bustle. Businessmen and women were thinning out, with the majority having left for their scheduled appointments, others for their flight, or wherever else they needed to be. Three meeting rooms were booked for seminars. The hotel staff was busily going about their business, while a few stragglers roamed the lobby. The humdrum was broken when an armoured car with two guards carrying shotguns, a strongbox, and an envelope entered the lobby.

Hank couldn't exactly remember all the details from the night before; he lay in bed with a perplexed expression on his face while Jackie was getting dressed. He remembered they had gone shopping, spending some of his impending fortune, borrowed from his father for now. He had bought her some clothes at Wal-Mart, even some sexy lingerie. He remembered they had spent the evening at home, drinking. He recalled her dancing naked, then drew a blank. He assumed they had sex, but couldn't recall.

Hank was now looking at Jackie over his hairy potbelly, grimacing while stroking a painful bump on his forehead. She slipped on her undergarments; he felt a twitch in his groin when she tucked her large breasts into her bra.

"Not so fast!" he ordered, while stroking his semi-hard genitalia.

Jackie turned and smiled at his interest. Their intended evening of debauchery had been cut short when he'd fallen and passed out after striking his head. She'd helped him up to the bedroom and he had collapsed onto the bed, where she let him be. From experience she knew it was best to let sleeping dogs lie.

Now he appeared to be in a fairly good mood, and the rising lump under the sheets appeared to confirm this. Letting her bra fall to the floor, she swayed back to the bed. Casting the sheets aside, his rising manhood was bared. Not wishing to let this opportunity pass, she took his cock into her mouth. Just then the phone rang; annoyed, he reached over to the night table and picked up on the second ring. It was Wincott.

Jackie had his cock unceremoniously pulled from her mouth when he quickly sat up. His uncharacteristic cordial mood quickly dissipated when he was informed that the trail leading to Martha was getting cold. Angrily he chastised Wincott, demanding to know what he was going to do now? Wincott assured him that he was on the case, and hoped to have some developments that day. After hanging up, Jackie attempted to resume her blowjob; impatiently Hank pushed her away, ordering her to make him breakfast.

Wincott sat back, pensively rubbing his chin. He had every intention of producing results that day, but was at a loss as to where to start. Obviously his attempt to deceive Martha and Marion backfired; he awaited their arrival in vain till the bank's offices closed. If the prey was now aware that it was being stalked, it would now be cautious and, as a result, harder to track. If only he could find out where they were staying. His best bet at this point was staking out Marion's apartment.

Although it was only mid-morning, Marion had already accomplished much. He was expecting the money transfer to occur momentarily. He had also put into play their getaway, contacting Mr. Vincent, who was more than happy to hear from Lloyd. Marion informed him that he had his money, plus interest, and asked if he was in a position to supply him with false identification quickly. Mr. Vincent confirmed that anything was possible for a price. When Mr. Vincent quoted seven thousand dollars each and Marion doubled the amount as well as clearing his gaming debt plus accumulated interest, Vincent wisely and promptly accepted the generous offer. Mr. Vincent invited Marion to drop off the cash to him so he could then direct him to the individual who could fulfill their need for the new identities.

A knock resounded at the door; Marion answered once he'd confirmed who it was. Martha, standing behind Marion, took a step back when she saw the intimidating armed guards at the door. Marion quickly invited them in, scanning the hallway up and down before closing the door.

Marion had made arrangements with the bank to have one hundred thousand dollars in varied denominations and a cashier's cheque for the balance of the 8.6 million delivered to them. Marion had the guards open the strongbox containing the cash. Martha gasped at the sight of the large quantity of money neatly stacked within. Each bundle of cash was secured with a paper band showing the amount it held.

Marion counted out the bundles, confirming the agreed amount, and signed for the delivery. Once that was accomplished, he had Martha conceal a couple of the bundles in her handbag while he counted out an amount and placed an envelope in his blazer breast pocket. The armed guards escorted them downstairs, where the hotel manager placed their remaining assets in the hotel safe.

Marion and Martha, with her bulging purse, hopped in a cab and directed the driver towards an area of town but not giving him a destination. At a subway stop, Marion ordered the driver to pull over, and generously compensated him. Then they both exited the cab and darted into the subway. They waited on the platform impatiently, again scanning everyone suspiciously; they barely spoke. Once on the train, they rode it for two stops before hailing a cab once they were above ground. Finally they arrived at their destination—a nondescript social club in the Italian area of the city.

Martha followed Marion into the bar trustingly. Once inside the dim, windowless hall, they stood motionless for a moment to allow their vision to adjust to the obscurity. Their senses were accosted by a multitude of sounds, smells, and loud voices. The cappuccino machine was steaming heads of frothy milk. Music from the speakers behind the bar blared, and ivory balls were breaking on the pool table. Soon all they could hear was silence, except for the stereo and the steam hissing from the coffee machine. Everyone in the place—old, young, short, tall, skinny, fat, grey-haired, longhaired, bald—all had stopped to stare at the two out-of-place individuals.

Marion stepped up to the bar and announced himself to the man behind it; with a wary scowl, the tough-looking, unshaven man bent down, reaching under the counter. A buzzing sound emanated from a metal windowless door at the back. The man indicated it with a motion of his head; Marion took Martha's hand and led her through the café. The patrons quickly resumed their routine once they saw that the two were expected. The men, old and young, all followed Martha admiringly with their eyes as she passed, many with smokes dangling from their lips.

Marion warily pushed open the door. Inside was Mr. Vincent and, standing next to him, the gentleman who had called on Marion earlier in the week. Mr. Vincent was leaning forward, his forearms resting on his desk, a blank stare on his face, his mouth a narrow slit; his cruel eyes spoke volumes.

Marion quickly pulled cash from his pocket as if in an attempt to appease a rabid animal. He placed the pre-agreed amount on the desk and slowly slid it towards his host. Mr. Vincent glanced down at the envelope momentarily before signalling his goon to count it. Upon his wordless invitation, both Marion and Martha sat across from him. He stared blankly at his two guests while his man counted the money. Once the agreed amount was confirmed, he picked up the phone and dialed a number from memory.

"Frank? Vincent. Listen, I have two clients for you, they need new suits . . . Yeah, ties, shirts, the whole bit. But they need it pronto—like today. Yeah, yeah, I know you're busy. Too busy for a big markup? Twice the regular price . . . Yeah, I thought you might just have an opening in your busy schedule. Yeah, I'm sending them right over. Do whatever needs to be done, the money's with me, we'll settle when we see each other."

After hanging up, Mr. Vincent gave them an address, with instructions to see his contact Frank. He assured them that he was the best, and just before they exited he waved the stack of bills above his head and bade them enjoy their new wardrobe.

Marion and Martha once again walked through the bar on their way out; again they were the focus of attention, but this time the atmosphere didn't pause for them. Once back out into the bright sunlight, Marion shielded his eyes in order to spot a cab. None was to be found. Glancing at the address he had been given, he saw it was only five blocks east from where they were. Hand in hand, they strolled down the avenue towards their next destination.

Wincott frowned pensively; he was behind the wheel of his car driving nowhere in particular for now. When he left his office after calling Hank Kowalski, he was planning to head for Marion Lloyd's apartment. He decided to take a detour; driving and thinking went hand in hand for him. He often wondered how he managed to get anywhere he was going without getting into, or causing, an accident, since he'd have little recollection of his drive. Once at his destination, if he had to recount which way he'd taken or what he'd seen on his way there, he'd be hard pressed for an answer.

Checking the addresses as he closed in on his target, he pulled over when he found it. There was a parking lot on one side of the building with a handful of cars parked in it. Lloyd's Jetta was not one of them; however, that didn't mean much. He called the apartment, making sure to block his number. He received no answer. Not wishing to waste a day sitting and waiting, he called his secretary. He had a hunch, which may or may not turn out to be a total waste of time. He instructed his assistant to call all four- and five-star hotels in the city in order to check if anyone by the name of Marion Lloyd or Martha Kowalski were checked in. He doubted they'd be staying at a cheap motel.

The printing shop was almost indiscernible from the street; it had a small sign on the door simply displaying "Pro Printing." The glass front was completely whitewashed. When he went to push the door open he found it locked. From an intercom box on the side of the brick wall, a tinny, distorted voice asked, "Yeah, who is it?"

Marion leaned in close, "Marion Lloyd. Mr. Vinc—" Before he could finish his sentence, they were buzzed in.

Inside, the musty smell of paper and pungent ink greeted them; from the back a balding man in his early thirties entered the front of the shop. He was very short, very slim, with dark, nervous, darting eyes. His physique was stringy; every muscle, sinew, vein, and nerve was visible under his seemingly paper-thin skin. Wiping his hands with a stained rag, he invited them to follow him into the rear of the shop. The back room seemed even more dirty and disorganized than the front. In a corner Marion saw a stool before a white backdrop facing a professional-looking instant camera on a tripod flanked by two flash assemblies.

The man, who never bothered to introduce himself, flipped through a filing cabinet, retrieving two folders. Pensively he glanced at the contents before addressing his clients. "If I understood right, you both want new identities, passports, driver's licenses, social security numbers etc." Marion and Martha nodded in unison. "Well, these are the new you," handing them each a folder.

Marion opened his; he saw a photo of a man approximately his age with flaming red hair and freckled face by the name of Andrew Robert

Finley. Martha opened hers to see a pretty, blonde young woman by the name of Margaret Ann Bellini. Martha turned to Marion, tilting the contents of her folder towards him.

"I don't look anything like her."

Smirking, the man answered her, "When I'm finished you still won't, but she'll sure look like you."

With that, he invited her to sit for a series of photos. He was certainly a professional at falsifying documents; he even had an assortment of clothing consisting of just tops. With each picture he had Martha—now a.k.a. Margaret—change tops, tie and untie her hair, even change her lipstick colour. He gave Marion—a.k.a. Andrew—different tops, including a blazer, shirt, and tie for one of the pictures. The purpose of the switches was to make it look as if the pictures had been taken on different occasions, lending them an air of authenticity. He even had the presence of mind to change the backdrop for each shot.

Thursday 3:53 p.m.

After the photo shoot Frank invited them to come back in a couple of hours to pick up their new identities. Once again Marion and Martha stepped out into the day's bright sunlight. They both walked around the front and crossed the street to a deli. Marion noted a travel agency conveniently located next door to it.

Wincott sat in his car watching Lloyd's building as well as the surrounding area in the hope of spotting his quarry, but to no avail. His cell phone rang, breaking the monotony; it was his secretary. She had found a Marion Lloyd staying at the airport Hilton. He sat up straight in his seat, his face flushed with joy, and, smiling, he thanked his girl, started the car, and sped towards the Hilton.

Hank waited for Wincott's call, his impatience festering, his anger even more intense since his recliner was missing. He sat uncomfortably on the sofa, staring blankly at the TV screen showing some mindless game show.

Jackie sat in the kitchen drinking coffee, herself staring blankly at the yellow walls of the small, bleak room. She had a bad headache from her excesses of the night before. Her mouth was dry and pasty; her stomach felt like it was full of lead. She was content with sitting alone in the kitchen filing her nails. She knew Hank was brooding in the living room, and she also knew to stay out of his way so he wouldn't direct his frustrations towards her. She now understood why his wife had picked up and left. She would have done the same if she had hit the jackpot. Actually if it was her, the *last* thing she'd want is a man. After a life of being beaten, sworn at, spit on, fucked and re-fucked by men, the last thing she needed was one of her own.

She'd probably live alone; her only use for men was for sex and security. Several million dollars would certainly take care of the security, while escorts would take care of her sexual needs. Leaning her head in her palm, she sipped her coffee while fantasizing; she pictured herself as she had looked in her prime, mid-twenties, wrinkle-free, slim, with a full, firm chest. Sitting in her parlour room drinking champagne in a flowing pink silk robe, *à la* Joan Crawford. A man would knock at her door; she'd invite him to come in. The door would swing open to reveal a classic, tall, dark, stunningly handsome man, a Chippendale kind of guy. He'd glide over to her in his black tuxedo, drop to one knee and take her hand in his, kissing it delicately.

He'd say she was the most beautiful woman in the world and that he couldn't go on without her and that he'd do anything to be with her. She'd turn her head away, explaining that he had to get over the infatuation he had for her, that he must content himself with shallow, meaningless sex. Her thought process quickly fast-forwarded to them being both naked on a giant canopy bed. Jackie cocked her head as she imagined his blue eyes staring up at her from between her open legs. She took another sip of her black coffee, her eyes staring blankly into space. She pictured him manipulating her pliable body with skill and gentleness. Exploring, probing every orifice. He had just penetrated her with his hard young cock when the phone's ringing snapped her out of her fantasy.

Hank picked up on the first ring, "It's about fuckin' time! Where are you? Did you find the cunt?"

Wincott listened at the other end, regretting having to deal with Hank Kowalski.

He allowed him to vent before continuing, "I managed to track her down. She's staying at a hotel in town," Wincott reluctantly informed him.

"Where? Give me the address!" Hank demanded excitedly.

"Now Mr. Kowalski, just knowing where she is doesn't solve the problem. I need to do more than just locate her—"

"Fuck that shit! I hired you to find her, and you did. Now give me the address!" Hank ordered.

"Mr. Kowalski—"

"NOW!" Hank shouted.

Wincott was silent for a moment. He knew that nothing good could come out of giving him the information; on the other hand, he was being paid by him and was at odds with holding back information.

"Mr. Kowalski, please consider the consequences of your actions," Wincott cautioned.

Hank hissed, "Where's my wife staying?"

"The airport Hilton—" Wincott said. The line went dead before he could continue.

Marion and Martha grabbed a quick bite at the deli before dropping into the travel agency. There, Marion requested a flight to South America, round trip, but their intention was not to come back. Once there, their new identities would kick in, and they would disappear. Having been assured that their plane tickets would be delivered by courier the next day by noon, they crossed the street back to the printer's to retrieve their new documentation.

Marion was truly impressed with the quality of the work. Every aspect of it appeared authentic, down to the lamination. The printer had thought of everything, down to weathering the surfaces of the cards so they appeared as if they had been handled; even the corners were worn and bent. He had marked the passports with a few airport stamps. Marion noted that Andrew Robert Finley had already travelled to France, Italy and Mexico, while Margaret Ann Bellini had only accompanied him to Mexico. Marion thanked the wayward printer profusely. From there, they hailed a cab to return to the hotel.

On the way, Marion contemplated their plans. He wished to return to his own apartment to retrieve some of his belongings, but weighed the risk and decided there was nothing of enough value to risk being seen. He could always wire some rent money to his landlord in order to keep his abode until they had a better perception of their plans.

Hank and Jackie arrived at the Hilton; Jackie exited the cab to marvel at the luxurious surroundings. Her contemplation was short lived when Hank, annoyed, rudely grabbed her arm and pulled her along. The man at the front desk observed them approaching, his face expressionless. He certainly observed that the two were out of place, but decorum prevented him from showing it.

"May I help you, sir?" the clerk politely asked.

"Yeah, I'm looking for Martha Kowalski," Hank stated.

"Is she a guest, sir?"

"No shit," Hank answered sarcastically. Jackie snickered at his rude remark.

The annoyed clerk turned to his monitor, punching in the name. After scrolling down his screen he replied, "I'm sorry sir, I don't show a Martha Kowalski."

Hank's hand, which was clasping Jackie's, tightened slightly. "Kowalski—K-O-W-A-L-S-K-I," he spelled out.

"Yes, sir, that's the way I entered it," the clerk politely replied.

"Try her maiden name—Martha Ingalls," Hank demanded.

The clerk again punched in the information, queried the monitor, and again came up negative. "I'm sorry, sir, but I don't show anyone by that name either."

Hank's hand gripped Jackie's tightly. She grimaced from the pain but held back any sign of protest for fear of escalating his anger.

Nervously running his hand through his greasy hair, "Maybe you've seen her, brown hair, plain, always carries a old black purse." Hank gestured, simulating gripping a handbag with his free hand.

"I'm sorry, sir, I can't say I've—" The clerk's response was cut short.

Hank slammed his fist on the counter, "I know she's here!"

The clerk quickly signalled a man by the elevators, who promptly made his way towards them. Hank, seeing the approaching security man in the blue blazer, pulled Jackie away, making his way to the exit.

"Fuck you, asshole," he yelled back while storming out.

Martha and Marion entered the lobby through the rotating doors at that exact moment. Martha stood stunned and paralyzed with fear when she spotted Hank. Ice ran through her veins as he approached her. Marion stood behind her; he froze in shock at seeing Martha's husband rushing towards them. Hank's eyes locked onto Martha's; she saw a combination of outrage, anger, and fury in them.

He closed in on her rapidly. She was so focused on him that her tunnel vision didn't even register the woman he was pulling behind him. She raised her hands to her face in a desperate attempt at self-preservation. She could smell Hank's rancid breath and perspiration, his grimacing face inches from her own. She braced herself for the imminent pounding he was going to administer. He slammed into her hard, and she fell to the floor. The security guard rushed over to assist. Martha attempted to shield herself from her attacker, kicking out in a desperate attempt at fending him off.

But Hank and Jackie flew past her, jumping into a cab! Hank had blasted right past her! Despite the fact that he had made direct eye contact, as well as colliding with her, he did not recognize her.

Marion, on his knees, held her tightly. In an attempt to bring her back to reality, he whispered in her ear, "He's gone, he's gone, he didn't recognize you . . . it's all right now, you're safe!"

She sobbed uncontrollably; Marion could feel her entire body tremble as he held her tightly. Marion reassured the guard as well as others now around them that they were fine. Martha slowly stood on trembling legs; she and Marion headed for the elevators. The security guard insisted on escorting them back to their room. Only once his two wards were safely in their suite did he take his leave.

Once the door was closed behind them, Martha broke down again. Marion sat beside her on the couch, hugging her tightly, "How did I do it?" she asked. "How did I live with him, how did I allow him to touch me? He's an animal." She raised her head, looking to Marion for an answer; but none came, only a kiss.

Hank barged into Wincott's office, "What the fuck am I paying you for?" Tipping over a chair.

Wincott's years of police work rose up quickly to take control of the situation. He looked at Hank sternly and in a controlled, even voice simply said,

"Pick up that chair and sit down, or get the fuck outta here while you can still walk."

Hank stopped dead in his tracks, flushing to a bright crimson red. He did as he was told, picking up the overturned chair and sitting down. Resentment was obvious in his face.

Wincott paused before continuing, just long enough to demonstrate he was in charge.

"You went to the hotel, didn't you?"

"She's my wife, I can do whatever I want. She wasn't registered," Hank pointed out.

"Maybe she's registered under the name of her companion?"

"Companion? *What* fuckin' companion?" he asked, shocked.

"I found the room under her *lawyer's* name, and he hasn't been back to his place for a while now. I suspect they're there together."

Hank's face went from bright pink to crimson red; he slid forward on the chair gripping the arms tightly. "They're together? You mean he's *fucking* her?"

Wincott raised his hand in a gesture of appeasement, "Now, hold on. I didn't say that. All I can confirm is that the lawyer in question seems to have set aside his practice in order to service your wife." Wincott regretted his choice of words; he should have known a man like Kowalski would twist what he just said.

"Service . . . service . . . fuckin' right he's servicing her. He's got eight million reasons to service her. He's fuckin' servicing her all right. He's probably servicing her up, down and sideways. He's probably fucking the living—"

Hank dropped to the floor in mid-sentence. Wincott stood looking at the man sprawled out on his office floor. He'd seen many a dead man in his day, and this man was dead.

Wincott yelled to his secretary to call an ambulance. Jackie, who had been sitting in the waiting room, ran in, and threw herself on the floor next to the body, shrieking wildly. Wincott debated if he should do CPR; the way the man fell he was certain his heart had exploded. Kowalski's face turned blue immediately. To his relief, Emily, his young secretary, ran in after calling 9-1-1 and began resuscitation. She checked his airway, listened for a heartbeat, then began to attempt breathing life into the man before applying chest compressions. He watched, impressed with the young girl's *savoir faire*; he then remembered that her CV had detailed the fact she had been a lifeguard during her summers in school.

Jackie was on her knees, clutching her hands nervously. She had stopped shrieking, and sat there silent, her mascara-streaked face a reflection of shock, staring at Hank's lifeless body.

Emily valiantly continued to try to breathe life into the man. She persisted till the paramedics arrived and took over. Quickly they transported him out of the office, rushing the gurney towards the elevator. Jackie followed in a daze.

When they had gone, all that was left was wrappings, swabs, and needle caps from the paramedics, along with a wet spot on Wincott's carpet. Judging from its location, it was probably urine from Kowalski's loss of body functions when he collapsed. Emily sat in one of the chairs leaning on one arm, her palm to her forehead. Wincott stood where he was when it all started, staring at where Hank had fallen.

"Mr. Wincott?"

The words broke his trance. "Huh? Yes . . . Oh . . . Yes, Emily?"

"Would you mind if I finish early today?" she asked.

"Of course. God, I mean yes, yes, you can. Actually I don't want you going home alone. I'll drive you," he offered.

"I'd appreciate that, Mr. Wincott."

Chapter 8

Martha asked Marion to make love to her. Her request seemed out of place; however, he complied wholeheartedly. She trembled beneath his touch; Marion wondered if it reflected fear or arousal. Nonetheless, he accommodated her, sliding his hand beneath her blouse, kneading her bosom. She returned his embrace with ardour, seemingly sublimating her feelings of dread through sex. Still clothed, and even before he realized it, she was upon him and he within her.

Martha rode his manhood aggressively, expressing her anger and fear coupled with extreme arousal. To all appearances it seemed as if she were frantically celebrating her survival from a potentially dangerous, if not deadly, encounter. She defiantly stared into Marion's eyes; humping him deliberately while he lay back captivated by her spell. Soon she climaxed, seeing her writhe in ecstasy sent him over the edge as well. For the longest while she lay atop him and they lay there holding one another tightly.

When the ambulance pulled up to the hospital emergency bay, a trauma team consisting of two doctors and three nurses awaited them. The ride over had been hectic, with the driver up front barrelling down city streets while the paramedic in the back detailed Hank's status over the radio to the hospital. Jackie sat up front trying to decipher what was being said. "Patient unresponsive" was the only thing she understood of the technical jargon that was being relayed. She looked back a couple of times but was unable to see Hank's face; with the technician frantically doing chest compressions, only his bare chest was visible, and it was still blue.

The waiting trauma team promptly took over from the ambulance team. The three nurses and the younger of the two doctors assumed the revival procedure, while the older doctor followed the stretcher in with the paramedic relating the circumstances to him. Jackie ran along behind Hank's entourage. She was stopped at the swinging doors of a room with a sign that read "Reanimation." From there, she was guided to a small room lined with chairs by one of the nurses and asked to wait there, assuring her that someone would be by to speak to her. Jackie didn't have to wait long; the older of the two doctors soon walked in, sat, and with a hand on her knee notified her that Hank had died from a massive coronary.

Wincott arrived shortly afterwards. When he inquired about Hank Kowalski, he was pointed towards the small room where Jackie was sitting. He had driven Emily home, having had to pull over a couple of times so she could vomit on the curb. He ordered her to get some rest, and said that he would call her with an update. When he walked into the room, Jackie was seated in one of the chairs, quietly staring at the floor.

"He's dead," she blurted out before Wincott even got the chance to ask.

He grimaced at the news before sitting next to Jackie, placing his arm around her shoulders. He knew now the right thing to do was to get in touch with Martha Kowalski and inform her of the unfortunate, or maybe for her, the fortunate turn of events.

Wincott drove Jackie home to her place. She asked what would happen now. He assured her he'd take care of the details and call her tomorrow. Pulling away, he decided the best course of action was to finally face the elusive Martha Kowalski.

Marion and Martha were getting ready for bed; the next day would be hectic, but before Marion could turn off his light the phone rang.

"Hello?" he asked suspiciously.

"Mr. Lloyd? There's a Mr. Wincott at the front wishing to speak to you, he says it's important."

"Who?" Marion asked, frowning. Their imminent escape was so close. "What now?" he thought.

"He says he has some very important information for you," the clerk related.

"Tell him you're mistaken, and I've checked out," Marion instructed.

From the background he heard a man's voice say, "Tell him Hank Kowalski is dead."

"Wait!" Marion interjected. A long pause ensued as Marion considered the information he'd just heard.

Wincott waited for a response. After an interminable pause, he was finally directed to a wing chair to the side of the lobby next to a small end table with a phone on it. Wincott picked up the receiver when it rang.

"Who are you?" Lloyd asked.

"Wincott. I'm a private detective hired to find Martha Kowalski. Hank Kowalski is . . . rather, was . . . my client. He had a massive coronary earlier today in my office . . ." Wincott paused, awaiting a response, but none came.

"I just wanted you to know that I know the circumstances of the situation and can understand why Mrs. Kowalski would want to distance herself from her husband."

Marion finally responded, "What hospital was he taken to?" he simply asked.

"University. If you wish, I can drive you down and we can iron out everything. I suspect Mrs. Kowalski was prepared to run; I just want her to know that won't be necessary now."

"Give me a few minutes," Marion instructed before hanging up.

Marion turned to find Martha sitting up in bed.

"Hospital?" she asked.

Marion didn't want to burden her with the information he'd just received, certainly not before verifying its validity.

"I've got to step out for a bit."

Martha grabbed his arm so quickly and firmly he winced from the pain, "NO! Not without me. Tell me what's going on."

Marion pried her manicured nails from his forearm. Holding both her hands, he looked at her pensively before saying,

"Honey, there's a piece of information I've got to verify before I burden you with it. I'll be back shortly."

"What information? Who's in the hospital?" she asked, a tear streaking down her cheek.

Marion put his face in his hands and breathed out audibly. Turning to Martha, he blurted out, "Hank may be dead."

Martha covered her mouth with both hands. Voluminous tears welled up in her eyes and cascaded down her face in a torrent when she closed them. Her chest convulsed with sobs. Marion placed his arm around her, feeling her tremble. She turned to look at him her face awash with tears, but when she pulled her hands away to speak he noted a hint of a smile.

"He's dead? Oh my God, he's dead!" she said with a mix of shock and glee.

"Whoa, sweetheart, I said he MAY be dead. I'm going to confirm it."

"Not without me," Martha stated.

When the elevator door opened, both Marion and Martha exited into the lobby. Wincott stood to greet them. Marion reluctantly shook Wincott's hand. Wincott realized the circumstances appeared suspicious and understood Lloyd's wariness. Wincott turned his attention to Martha, introducing himself. Judging from Hank Kowalski's appearance he'd expected Martha to be a meek, unattractive and abused woman. He hadn't expected the vision that stood before him. Once the introductions were done, Wincott offered to drive, but Marion firmly suggested they'd best take a cab.

On the way to the hospital, Marion questioned Wincott, who sat up front while they sat in the back of the cab.

"What's your interest in this?" Marion asked directly.

"At this time, none other than to inform you of the events. My client is dead; I knew Mrs. Kowalski didn't have children, her parents are dead, and if she'd leave she'd probably never return. Consequently, she'd probably never know. Once we leave the hospital, my job is done."

Marion acknowledged this with a nod, and the rest of the ride was quiet. Martha sat quietly in the rear of the cab. Following her outburst of sentiment when she was told of Hank's supposed death, she withdrew emotionally, keeping quietly to herself. During the cab ride she hardly looked at the others; she sat gazing pensively out her window. She was still reeling from the week's events, and now she was slapped with her husband's death. Strangely, she felt as if she had been informed of a distant relative's passing.

Even though she was sleeping with him only a few days ago, and ran into him face to face only hours ago, she felt miles away from the man. Emotionally she was unmoved by the news; only the prospect of being rid of her tormentor touched her. She regarded it as enduring a chronic illness her whole life and finally being purged of it.

If what Wincott was saying was true, and not some kind of ruse, Marion certainly welcomed Hank's death. Once confirmed, were they in the clear? Did Hank have a will? If he did and Martha was the beneficiary, then yes, they were. If he didn't and he had other surviving relatives, then no, they weren't.

His thoughts were interrupted by their arrival at the hospital. Once inside, they inquired at the desk and, once Martha had identified herself as the deceased's wife, they were escorted by an attendant to the morgue. Marion was relieved that all seemed to confirm what Wincott had told him was true.

Wordlessly they rode the elevator to the hospital's sub-basement. When the doors opened, the glare of the sterile neon lighting made them

Tia Doré **85**

squint. Only the sounds of the humming fixtures and their footsteps on the tile floors were audible. The attendant made them wait in front of a large glass windowpane, informing them that he'd wheel the corpse on the other side so that Martha could view the body.

The tension was palpable; Martha and Marion stood nervously. Both involuntarily took a step back when the curtains behind the glass pane were drawn open. There lay a body beneath a white sheet. Martha knew it was Hank even before the attendant revealed the cadaver. Many a night she lay awake staring at him as he lay on his back snoring. The profile beneath the sheet was exactly that of Hank's. The attendant drew back the sheet, and there he lay: one eye slightly opened, his mouth partially agape, the body ashen gray, the lips a bluish hue. Martha stared at him for a moment before nodding a confirmation. Marion put his arm around her shoulder; the woman was as rigid as the corpse before them.

Wincott stood in the background; he preferred to be an observer rather than a participant. The curtains closed, and Martha stood unmoving, as though there were something still there to see, and Marion continued to hold her. The door opened, and the attendant beckoned to them to follow him. Back upstairs, papers were signed, arrangements made, with Martha promising to have the body claimed within twenty-four hours. Marion weighed in his mind the turn of events; would their plans still be justified or even necessary? After all, they were to fly out Saturday afternoon, and it was already Thursday night. Once all was done, the three of them boarded a cab to return to the hotel. There Wincott bade them farewell, after leaving his card with them. His work on this case seemed done.

Friday 8:47 a.m.

Jackie stood before the white picket fence that was in desperate need of a fresh coat of paint. The house was from the post-war era, and nothing she could see showed any modern countenances. Original windows, original stone walkway, even the rusty steel mailbox appeared original. The lawn was weed-strewn and parched from lack of watering. She was there to inform Mr. Kowalski of the loss of his son.

Her eyes were puffy from being up half the night pondering how to inform Hank's father of his son's passing. Her recent experience of meeting him was less than inspiring; as a matter of fact, it had been truly frightening. She now knew where Hank got his mean streak. While she stood just outside the gate, the house's front door opened, and she watched Hank Kowalski Senior step outside. The ancient screen door creaked loudly on its wooden frame supported by sagging rusty spring-hinges. Without glancing about, he bent over, picked up the paper on his stoop, and turned to go inside. Halfway in, he paused. Almost as an afterthought, he turned to look at the figure in front of his house. Jackie stood motionless in anticipation of a chastising, which never came.

She had dressed more solemnly this morning. Instead of her usually loud, colourful clothing, she had toned down her appearance, opting for a subdued maroon low-cut sweater and black skirt; although the skirt was shorter than what would be considered appropriate, it was far more acceptable than her usual attire. She had worn only lipstick with a little eyeliner instead of the customary heavy makeup.

"What is it?" he called out to her.

"Sir, I have something to tell you . . . It's important." She raised her voice so he could hear her.

"Well unless the neighbours need to hear also, maybe it's best if you come in." With that, he stepped inside.

Jackie hurriedly unlatched the gate, stepping briskly up the walkway to the stoop, surprised at his invitation. Once at the door, she paused to tug at her skirt and smooth out her clothing before yanking the screen door open to step inside. An empty hallway and the smell of brewing coffee heavy in the air greeted her.

"In here," he bellowed.

She found him in the kitchen pulling a second cup from the kitchen cupboard. He inspected it to verify its cleanliness before setting it onto the counter next to his.

"Coffee?" he asked without turning.

Jackie, surprised at the invitation to join him, quickly replied, "Yes, please!"

He filled the two mugs. "Yesterday I was a little beside myself. I owe you an apology."

Jackie's eyes opened wide, her head raised back slightly in surprise.

"Oh, that's okay, I understand . . . I guess."

He set one of the cups before Jackie, and after placing the cream and sugar on the table he took his place. Confidently he crossed his legs, leaning back in his seat.

"So what made you brave a return trip?" he asked with a slight glint in his eyes.

"Sir, I . . . I came to tell you, inform you that—" she began. A tear formed, cascading down her cheek.

Hank Sr. picked up a paper napkin from the holder, handing it to her, a concerned frown on his sun-bronzed face.

"I'm sorry, I don't . . . Hank died last night," she blurted before burying her face in her hands and sobbing.

After a moment she lifted her head and, through tear-soaked eyes, refocused on her host. He sat unmoved, his position and expression unchanged except for a slight cocking of the head indicating disbelief.

"Dead? Hank? How?" he asked.

Jackie recounted the events of the previous day in Wincott's office. She avoided Hank Sr.'s piercing eyes, looking down at the floor throughout the narrative. When she had finished, Hank Sr. reached over to touch her face. Jackie jerked back in surprise. Hank Sr. gave her a knowing look.

"He beat you, didn't he?" he asked directly.

"Yes, sometimes," she replied, embarrassed.

"He got that from me, I'd hit his mother. She died when he was just a boy from a brain tumour. Been a widower for the past thirty years. I swore I'd never hit another woman, never did since then . . . Never had another woman since then, though."

Hank Sr. propped his elbows on his thighs. Staring at the floor he sighed before continuing.

"Hank was our only child. I was a terrible father and I demanded a lot from him. Some kids are born with certain attributes, talents, strong points, if you will. Hank didn't have any. He didn't excel in school, didn't have friends, never participated, no team spirit. Unfortunately he was 'always right,' knew everything, as such he never wanted to learn. He repelled everything. While kids his age were like a sponge for knowledge, as kids should be, Hank was a rock—hard, unyielding.

"As he grew, so did his attitude. We fought often; hell . . . always. He grew up stubborn and stupid; the only good fortune he ever had was to marry a woman who was as meek as he was headstrong. Martha would do whatever he asked. Problem was, she was too good a woman for him, too trusting. I guess everything has to balance in the end. He rode her hard; now he's dead and she's far better off without him."

He raised his eyes to look at Jackie.

"I guess you got a taste of my mean streak when you were here. It's all due to the culmination of an unhappy life, a life full of mistakes and regrets."

Jackie leaned forward, placing her hand on his. Just then the phone rang. Hank Sr. picked up the receiver.

"Hello? Martha, God, yes, I know . . . I just found out. Yes, of course, no, no. Of course you're welcome . . . I'm here." After a pause he continued, "Who, your lawyer . . . I guess, that's fine . . . No, he's my son, the least I can do is bury him . . . We'll talk when you get here."

Hank Sr. hung up, he stood staring at the phone a moment before turning and sitting back down. Jackie again took his hand. Hank Sr. squeezed it in return, and then he asked,

"What threw Hank over the edge in the detective's office?"

"Well, Hank and Mr. Wincott were discussing Martha, and Mr. Wincott brought up the fact that Hank's wife was sharing a room and probably sleeping with her lawyer. That's when Hank pulled a fit, screaming, then he just . . . dropped."

Hank Sr. straightened up in his chair. A perplexed look came over his face, with a hint of suspicion, "Really?"

Martha hung up with Hank Sr. and she was relieved, as well as surprised, at his levelheaded response. Marion stood next to her. With his hand on her shoulder, he counselled, "Honey, going to see him may not be a good idea."

She looked up at him questioningly, "Why?"

"Well, you've told me he's a wise old man, money hungry and a miser. We know that he knows you've won a lottery, and he's his son's only survivor."

Martha gazed up at Marion blankly; unaware of the point he was trying to make. Marion bent down, taking her hand in his, he clarified.

"Sweetheart, he probably knows the law. Your husband has no sibling or living relatives besides his father. He's entitled to half of his son's assets. That includes half the winnings."

Martha's eyes dropped.

"We're back to square one."

"I'm afraid so."

Marion paused to let Martha contemplate the options; then added,

"It's all arranged, Martha. Tomorrow we can still board a plane and disappear; you leave all your problems behind, we start a new life . . . together."

The word "together" seemed to trigger an emotional reaction in her. Teary-eyed, she hugged Marion, saying simply,

"You're right, Sweetheart!"

Friday 10:02 a.m.

Jackie had made some breakfast; Hank Sr. sat at the table while she went back and forth from the fridge to the stove, to the table and back again. Making eggs, toast with jam, bacon, and fresh coffee, she whipped up a meal a single man rarely takes the time to make for himself. Hank Sr. observed her shuffling about, bending over, and her ample bosom jiggling as she whipped the eggs. Her short skirt was riding up her thighs. A widower for over two decades and not having had a woman in all that time was suddenly obvious from the look of the crotch of his pants.

Although in his late fifties and bald, he still had a slim, spry physique. His face showed its age, but his body reflected a man in his mid-forties. Not being a drinker or smoker, he was far healthier than his late son had been. The woman he abhorred yesterday suddenly looked very appealing. She was attractive; far more appealing with modest makeup than the painted whore perception he got from her the last time she was there. She sat next to him once the table was all set and the food laid out. She beamed a smile at him, a sincere, kind smile he'd never have thought her capable of. They had an exceptionally pleasant time, talking, laughing, and enjoying each other's company.

Jackie found him down to earth, and surprisingly kind, far more so than his son. She tried to recall Hank smiling or laughing, but couldn't. He never had; his face was a permanent frown, reflecting hate, suspicion, mistrust. His eyes were cruel and unfeeling, like a predatory animal. His face had been devoid of laugh lines, his forehead creased by frown lines only. His father, on the other hand, although similar, was capable of shedding the rough exterior to show a sensitive side. In her eyes he seemed to get younger by the minute, and attractive, in a way.

She learned that following a work-related accident shortly after his wife's death, he was awarded a substantial insurance settlement, which he wisely invested; it had been supporting his modest lifestyle ever since.

Jackie sat, her chin poised in her palm, her elbow resting on the table. Her body language spoke volumes. She leaned forward, her legs turned toward her host; a look of fascination displayed on her face. Her clear blue eyes glinted with interest.

A knock was heard at the door. Hank Sr. rose to answer it, expecting to find Martha with her friend. Instead, a cabdriver stood there holding a plain brown manila envelope.

"Sir, this is for you." The driver promptly handed him the envelope before taking his leave.

Perplexed, Hank Sr. scrutinized the envelope, then walked back to the kitchen with it. Sitting down, he picked up a clean knife and cut open the flap. Reaching in, he withdrew a stack of bills. Jackie's mouth dropped open when she saw what it contained. Then he did what came naturally: he counted it. It came to ten thousand dollars. He set down the money, and, leaning back in his seat, he contemplated it.

"What's that for?" Jackie asked, surprised.

"To soothe their conscience," Hank replied pensively.

Wincott's cell phone rang, and he pondered before answering it. It had been a hell of a week and he didn't recognize the number. He was on his way to the golf course and his tee-off was in twenty minutes, but curiosity got the best of him. He regretted answering the moment he realized who it was.

"Mr. Wincott? It's Jackie Daniels, I'm with Hank's father; he wants to talk to you." Wincott whipped off his golf cap and threw it on the seat next to him in exasperation before pulling over.

As calmly as he could, he answered, "Yes, Miss Daniels."

An even-toned man's voice came on the line.

"Mr. Wincott? My name is Hank Kowalski Senior. I understand my son hired your services and left you with a retainer."

"Yes, he did, Sir, and Monday I will deduct my fee and return the balance to you," Wincott promised.

"That won't be necessary Mr. Wincott. I'll be retaining your services on my son's behalf."

Wincott winced at the suggestion. "Mr. Kowalski, my responsibility in this case ended with your son's death."

"Correction, Mr. Wincott. Your responsibility was to investigate and report. The one you reported to can't act on the information you supplied.

He's dead," Hank Sr. reminded Wincott. "Let's say we get together and go over the details of this situation and draw your investigation to an adequate close."

Wincott sighed. "Where and when?"

"ASAP at your office, Mr. Wincott."

Information was exchanged between the two parties before Wincott put the car back in gear. With another sigh he merged back into the traffic. His tee-off would have to wait.

Chapter 9

Martha nervously put together a suitcase. She'd have to leave behind many of the outfits she'd recently acquired. Although she wished to take them all with her, she understood the necessity of travelling light. Marion had bought her a Samsonite similar in style to the ones stewardesses use—compact and functional. She'd never flown; the combination of embarking into the unknown as well as going there by plane unnerved her. There always seemed to be something that would set back her confidence; this was again such an event. Bent over trying to zip up her bag Marion slipped behind her. With his arms encircling her waist, he kissed the back of her neck and whispered reassuringly, "Relax, you won't be alone, we're in this together."

Martha wiggled her way out of his hold.

"I hope this is the right thing to do, I feel that we'll be running like fugitives forever. It seems everyone is after us," she lamented.

"It's a big world; besides, it's not as if we killed someone, we didn't do anything wrong."

Martha looked at him downhearted. "I hope not."

A Swiss bank with a branch in the Caribbean gladly agreed to accept the funds. Marion had all transactions made through Martha's new identity now that they had all the backup identification in place. He felt confident of his plan: He and Martha were going to fly into Buenos Aires under their real names, where they would switch to their new identities before proceeding to their final destination via a private charter. Anyone tracking them would lose their scent in Argentina.

The route to the airport was short; within minutes they were at the airline counter. Martha was fidgeting nervously while Marion checked them in. Marion noticed a slight tremor in his own hand while handing the young lady at the airline counter their tickets. Marion prayed his well-laid-out plan would go off without a hitch. He took Martha's sweaty palm once they had checked in; walking hand in hand, they headed for their departure gate.

Hank Kowalski Sr. opened the weathered wood garage door. The gloom of the windowless shelter was broken by the midsummer sun streaming in. The walls of the single-car garage were cluttered with boxes, an old bike, and various tools hanging from a pegboard. Among the clutter was a tarp-covered car. Hank Sr. pulled the cloth off the vehicle, revealing a metallic navy blue 1972 Chevy Impala two-door sedan in pristine condition. The bumpers gleamed in the bright sunlight. Hank Sr. stepped around to the passenger side, opening the door for Jackie. She smiled at his considerate action, taking her place on the front bench seat. The vinyl seat squeaked beneath her buttocks. The car smelled slightly musty; however, the interior was immaculate. Hank Sr. stepped around, taking his place in the driver's seat, and closed the heavy door with a thud.

The engine came to life immediately when he cranked it. The motor rumbled confidently. Hank Sr. let the large V8 turning under the long hood warm up for a minute before kicking off the choke. Placing his arm over the back of the seat he backed out of the carport before securing the garage door. The potent car pulled into the quiet street with a throaty rumble. Jackie glanced at the odometer; it displayed 22,000 kilometres, and she wondered if it was 122,000 kilometres, or maybe even 222,000 kilometres. Judging from the car's showroom condition she concluded it was surely an extremely low-mileage vehicle. The car suited Hank Sr.: although old, it conveyed a sense of exceptionally good condition for its age. She would shortly learn that her assumption was justified.

Hank Sr. found parking right in front of the building where Wincott's office was situated. He exited his door before dashing nimbly around to Jackie's side. There he took hold of her hand and assisted her out of the car. Jackie blushed at his attention; she even gave a small curtsy in response to his gentlemanly act. Hank Sr.'s considerate behaviour came late in life: in his youth and throughout his marriage he was much like his son, verbally and physically abusive towards his wife and only child. It must have been the opportunity for contemplation during his many years as a widower that had reformed him.

Years of loneliness had turned him into a frustrated miser. Now that he had a woman accompanying him for the first time in over two decades, he felt like a young man again. His heart palpitated the entire drive down in Jackie's company. He was using facial muscles he had forgotten were there. He stepped lightly; his ego was bolstered by the simple fact that Jackie still held his hand while walking into the building.

Inside, a sign indicated, "Wincott Investigative Services 2ⁿᵈ floor." He politely invited Jackie to take the lead up the stairs. Walking behind her he was treated to the sight of Jackie's rump sensually swaying side to side as she climbed up the steps. With each riser her skirt rose ever higher up her thighs till he could see the white of her panties. Reaching the midpoint of their climb he boldly took her hand, spinning her around to him taking her in his arms. She was both startled and flattered by his bold advance; yet she offered no resistance. Coyly she looked into his eyes, blushing, her lips parted slightly in a coy smile when she felt Mr. Kowalski's member pressing insistently against her lower belly.

"Mr. Kowalski! There's a time and a place for this, you know."

Hank Sr. pulled her tightly to him; he pressed her against the wall of the stairwell. Squeezed between him and the wall, Jackie returned his daring advance. Their lips locked, tongues exploring enthusiastically. Jackie's hand rubbed the front of his pleated slacks, which displayed his willing erection. Her eyes widened in surprise at his level of arousal; his penis felt huge. He felt harder than his son had and far larger. While he groped at her sweater, lifting it over her breasts, she unzipped him. Hank Sr. surprised Jackie with his strength when he lifted her up against the wall.

Her legs locked around his thin waist, her arms wrapped around his shoulders. Hank Sr. slid his hand between their trembling bodies; he skillfully slid her panties aside before thrusting himself in her. In unison they exclaimed their arousal out loud. Jackie received his every thrust with abandon. His strong, nimble body held her firmly against the wall as they fucked wildly. Jackie was the willing recipient of years of built-up sexual frustration, and she allowed him to hump her mercilessly. She felt bad thinking it, but if his son had fucked her with such dynamism, she thought, "To hell with the money."

Although they were barely at it for a minute, both received gratification. Hank Sr. gently set Jackie back down on her feet. Once done, he replaced his still firm member back into his pants. Jackie quickly straightened out her clothing, ran her hands through her hair and with a hand on each breast adjusted her bosom. Out of breath and panting, they both resumed their ascent to Wincott's office.

In the quiet, semi-commercial building, Wincott sat at his desk catching up on some paperwork while awaiting Kowalski's arrival. Through his open office doorway he heard the main entrance door in the lobby open, followed by footfalls coming up the stairwell. Anticipating their arrival, he straightened his desk. Moments later he heard what sounded like a man and woman having sexual relations. With a frown he cocked his head towards the out-of-place sounds. He was certain his assumption was correct when at one point he overheard a female voice cry, "Yes, oh God, yes!" This went on for a minute or so before the echoing footsteps resumed.

Before long, Jackie and Hank Kowalski Sr.—who sported a distinct wet spot on the crotch of his trousers—stood before him. Hank Sr. stepped forward, offering his hand in greeting. Wincott shook it with aversion when he realized Hank's palm was damp. Offering them both a seat, he took the time to wipe his hand with a tissue before sitting down himself.

Friday 2:57 p.m.

Martha had followed Marion's lead till then. Checking in, passing through security, taking a seat at their gate awaiting the call to board. She observed the aircraft with awe through the picture window. She'd never seen an airplane from this close; it appeared huge. All her life, she had never even been to an airport . . . never needed to . . . she never went anywhere, at least not before now. When their row was called, she followed Marion anxiously. A pleasant uniformed young woman checked their tickets and invited them to proceed down a windowless, curving hall. They descended the tube structure till a left turn led them to what appeared to be an open vault door. Inside stood another smiling young woman flanked by a cheerful uniformed man. Marion gave them their boarding passes for their review.

"Business class row 3, seats A and B, right there, sir," the woman pointed out pleasantly.

Martha looked at the plane's interior with awe. It appeared as sterile as an operating room, with plastic and glass dominating. The first few rows of seats were wide, leather-upholstered and plush; beyond a divider were seemingly endless rows of multicoloured paisley seats, narrower and in threes on each side.

Her breathing suddenly felt laboured, her heart raced. She unwittingly turned in a bid to escape, but other passengers now boarding behind them blocked her exit. The male steward turned, concerned, just as Marion grasped her arm.

"She's fine, it's her first time," Marion informed the young man.

Marion gently took her by the elbow and guided her to their seats. He sat her next to the window seat, while he took the aisle seat—not so much in courtesy, but more as a precaution in case she tried to bolt again. He put his arm around her and brought her head to his chest. "There's nothing to worry about, honey. I've flown many times. This will become routine to you," he reassured her.

Martha observed the long line of boarding passengers. Young, old, couples, children, were filing past her. She took comfort in the fact that there would be so many flying along with them. Once the boarding was complete, her state of nervousness increased when the crew closed the hatch. Her only route of escape was gone.

Strange noises invaded the passenger compartment, bumping, electric whining sounds, thumping. She looked at Marion questioningly, but asked nothing of him when she didn't detect any nervousness from him or the other passengers. The plane soon backed away from the terminal. It then turned and advanced, lumbering towards the runway.

"Don't be frightened—we'll be taking off soon," Marion said, squeezing her hand.

Slowly her confidence strengthened. *After all, it doesn't seem much different than a bus ride.*

The pleasant young man who had greeted them now gave instructions for every one of the emergency procedures, and pointed to the exits as well as demonstrating what seemed to be a child's inflatable pool toy as a life preserver. This did little to put her at ease. After a few turns, the plane came to a halt, and Martha once again lifted her head to scrutinize the other passengers, who appeared oblivious to anything worthy of alarm. Her shortness of breath quickly returned and her heart started thumping alarmingly when a shudder went through the airplane as the engines aggressively accelerated. She was close to tears when Marion took his arm away from her shoulders to sit up straight in his seat. He kept her hand in his.

The plane thrust forward, propelled by its huge engines. The ride became decidedly rougher as the aircraft gained speed. She glanced out her window at the fleeting landscape. The "G" forces insistently pressed her into her seat. She couldn't recall ever moving this fast. Her hand gripped Marion's; he tried to betray no pain as her fingernails gouged into his hand. Her other hand gripped her armrest just as hard. As fast as they were moving, she was certain they couldn't move any faster, but the plane relentlessly accelerated. She gasped when she felt the nose rise into the air, a quick glance out the window confirming they were pointed skyward. Before she could react, she felt the behemoth leave the ground. She felt a momentary sensation of suspension before the powerful aircraft seemed to take control and propel itself skywards. Her fear was quickly replaced by astonishment as the earth dropped away from them. After they reached an altitude that left all but large landmarks indistinguishable, her fear abated slightly. Looking at Marion with relief she sighed,

"We made it."

Wincott found Kowalski Sr. far more civil than his late son, and Jackie seemed to be in a world of her own. Her head turned to the side, seemingly fixated on a recently cleaned spot on the carpet where barely twenty-four hours earlier lay her last lover. Wincott surveyed Jackie with some distaste at the thought of the two of them copulating with abandon in public while his son— her lover—lay on a slab in the morgue.

Hank Sr. spoke.

"Mr. Wincott, my proposal is simple, I understand you've done some legwork already on finding my son's wife." Wincott let him continue. "Whatever you've uncovered or discovered, I'd like you to bring this situation to a close."

Wincott interrupted, "Mr. Kowalski, I owe you some money your son gave as a retainer. I've deducted the amount owed to me, and am refunding the rest with this cheque to you. With that my involvement is concluded."

Kowalski eyed the envelope Wincott slid towards him. "That's all very well and good, but the man who could benefit from your services is dead. Whatever you dug up is now futile. What I'm asking from you is to pursue your assignment to a close. And what I consider closed is having Martha pay me what she owes my son." Hank Sr. slid the envelope back across the desk to Wincott.

Wincott paused in consideration before responding.

"All right, here's what I know so far . . ."

Wincott recited what he knew to date, leaving out the part where he accompanied both Martha and her lawyer/lover to the hospital. Hank Sr. asked Wincott to make sure all was still as it had been till he contacted the lawyer on Monday.

Satisfied with his meeting with Wincott, Hank Sr. and Jackie left for their next destination.

Friday 3:41 p.m.

Martha's anxiety subsided; she was now beginning to enjoy the lavish service they were being treated to in first class. First they were offered champagne with fresh strawberries, followed by assorted canapés, and finally a well-appreciated meal of steak and mixed vegetables. When the stewards were picking up, Martha unwound by reclining her seat. The flight was remarkably smooth. She now felt silly at the way she had acted when they boarded. Marion looked over at Martha as she lay back with her eyes closed, a discreet smile on her face; he wondered what she was thinking. This was a well-appreciated reprieve from the hectic week that had just passed.

Marion had planned to ask her once they reached their final destination, but the moment seemed right. Reaching into his jacket's breast pocket he retrieved a small box. Opening it, he shielded it from Martha's view while he inspected the glittering two-carat diamond in a white gold setting. He had no remorse for the way he had acquired the twenty-five-thousand dollar ring. He had made a down payment by maxing out his credit card, and financed the rest with the jewellery store situated off the hotel lobby. Essentially, he knowingly stole it, since he had absolutely no intention of making the payments. His credit card bill would never be paid and his financing agreement was a scam, since once they landed, Marion Lloyd would no longer exist.

He leaned towards Martha; momentarily he stared at her serene, sleeping face. He didn't love her, not yet anyway; he wondered if he would at some point. Marion had never truly loved anyone. The few relationships he'd had were short-lived and tumultuous, much like his parents' marriage. Marion didn't come from a broken marriage, but it would have been a blessing if he had. His parents were socialites; both came from affluent families. Their union was not their choice, but their families'. Americans scoff at societies that arrange marriages. Societies that auction off their offspring to other families in exchange for influence, social acceptance, livestock even. The American belief is that of freedom of choice, the all-consuming pursuit for true love; but the truth is often far removed from those ideals. The American divorce rate is one of the highest in the world, but his parents never appeared in that statistic. They chose to remain united in their persecution of their only son.

Marion strove to please his parents. He was a good-looking, bright boy who had the abilities to exert himself at anything he undertook; however, whatever he accomplished qualified as passable but never stellar. He did enjoy the good things in life and always managed to come up with the goods in order to achieve his goals. His father never forgave him for not sticking with the law firm he'd used his contacts to open their doors to him, and deciding instead to go on his own. His father once paid him a surprise visit to his office when he had first opened his one-man practice. Marion still recalls vividly the disdain on his father's face when he saw where and how his son had set up shop. His father simply turned and walked away. He'd never again asked Marion about his work. As a matter of fact, after Marion showed up at one of his parents' functions driving his beat-up Volkswagen, his father had the butler drive it around back of the guesthouse so the other guests wouldn't wonder who owned the less-than-flattering vehicle.

His father, a noted physician, kept contact with him to a minimum after that. Marion was certain his father knew of his penchant for gambling. He'd never mentioned it to Marion, but he rarely discussed things that were distasteful to him. His father was not one to partake of confrontation, preferring to ignore Marion when displeased with him.

Marion had a knack for somehow walking on the edge; his rent money always came up at the limit of his landlord's tolerance. His bills were always overdue but somehow always eventually paid. His credit cards were always maxed out but never suspended. Marion somehow always came up with the goods one way or another. This bolstered his confidence to the point of cockiness.

For the last while, he'd been totally ignored by his parents to the point where he hadn't even been invited to any of the family functions other than Christmas dinner. His mother also distanced herself from him after his numerous breakups with daughters of friends she'd matched him with. He'd pretty well burned all his bridges with his parent's affluent friends after he'd dated several eligible young women and managed to betray every relationship. He never saw a future, never really caring for any of his unfortunate conquests. Soon his playboy image assured that he'd never gain anyone's trust again—in that circle, anyway.

Till now Martha had been still more of a client than anything else. She had come a long way from just a few days ago, to the point where it seemed hard to believe he'd known her for such a short time. He'd decided to propose, again not so much out of love but out of security for his interests in Martha's assets. His hope was that love for her would eventually rise to the surface. Before her transformation from ugly duckling, he'd never even have considered marrying or even having sex with her. But now he could think of worse fates.

He'd had far better lovers than she, but he was kind enough to understand the circumstances, and hoped her lovemaking would eventually evolve from mechanical to passionate. Meanwhile, he leaned over to gently kiss her lips; her large auburn eyes came to life. Acknowledging him, she beamed a bright smile. Marion held his hand up to her eyes, and for a moment she strained to focus on what he was holding before her. Once her eyes became accustomed, she mouthed a silent "ahh!"

Sitting up, she took the ring box from him; looking back and forth from him to the ring, she shook her head in disbelief. Taking the ring from the box, Marion slid it onto her finger. Slightly large, it kept sliding to the side of her finger from the weight of the massive rock.

"Will you marry me?" he murmured.

Tears formed in Martha's eyes. Wiping one that streamed down her cheek she said, "I can't—I'm already married."

Marion inappropriately smiled coyly. "Really? I thought you were a widow."

A shudder went through Martha as if she had just come to the realization, raising her hand to her forehead as though she were dazed.

She had been unsure of Marion till that point. She'd always lived by the adage that first impressions are usually the correct ones. Her first encounter with Marion had been less than impressive; however, he'd been an indispensable support these past few days. She would have been totally lost without his guidance in coping with the week's whirlwind of events. His patience in her regard was also reassuring, and now she needed him more than ever, 30,000 feet in the air heading into the unknown at 600 miles per hour.

"Yes, I will!" she answered before kissing him passionately.

Once back in the car, Hank Sr. and Jackie were unable to keep their hands off each other. Behaving like horny teenagers they groped and fondled each other while pulling away from the office building. Jackie was crouched down in the passenger seat. Panties around her ankles she allowed Hank Sr. liberal access to her womanhood. She in turn fondled his eager shaft. Both were in a heightened state of arousal. Jackie again marveled at the man's stamina, she never would have thought a man his age would be capable of rebounding from the exertion he'd sustained barely an hour ago.

Jackie climaxed again in the parking lot of the funeral home. They had to sit for several minutes in the car as Hank Sr. waited out a stubborn erection. Finally he had it moderately under control, enough anyway so the ample cut of his pants camouflaged it reasonably well. Exiting the car, it was Jackie's turn to sport a distinct wet spot on the back of her skirt from the pool of her juices, which had trickled down during their quickie.

They tried to maintain protocol, stepping into the home's lobby. The funeral director greeted them solemnly, offering them the rudimentary condolences on their loss. Jackie was introduced as a family friend. Taking a seat in the director's office they politely declined the offer of coffee. Both appeared anxious to get things settled. The director perceived that they were pressed for time. Hank Sr. ordered a simple service; he chose an unadorned, inexpensive pine box. Stated his wish that it be a closed casket ceremony and informed the gentleman that he had a plot purchased next to his wife at the Glengarry Cemetery, and wished to have his son interred there. He ordered a private ceremony and gave the director the necessary information. Once times were confirmed, they took their leave.

Back in the car, they resumed their assault on each other. Only Hank Sr. was visible in the car as Jackie fellated him. His hand fondled her pendulous breasts while her head bobbed in his lap. Hank Sr. did his best to concentrate on his driving, despite the enormous distraction he was contending with. A few welcome turns later he pulled into his driveway; contrary to his habit, he left his car outside. Both exited the vehicle and ran into the house.

Hank Sr. crouched forward in an attempt to hide his blatant erection straining his pants. Jackie was less concerned with appearances; simply pulling her top back down to conceal her exposed breasts she ran with her skirt hiked up around her waist. Her left foot had a shoe on while her right foot was bare; her panties were looped around her right ankle, trailing along the ground with each wobbly step. Hank Sr. fumbled with his keys, hoping none of the neighbours were witnessing the spectacle. The door swung inward, and both stumbled in. Jackie bolted up the stairs giggling, while Hank Sr. ran behind her, cradling her buttocks and guiding her towards the bedroom.

Both leaped upon the double bed, desperately shedding their clothing as if on fire. Once they were both in the buff, Hank Sr. plunged into Jackie with abandon. Having received his reward not long before his vigour was prime for the deed, Hank Sr. released a moan of satisfaction, while Jackie exclaimed a yelp of pleasure.

Jackie received him appreciatively; she was no stranger to fornication—whether one-on-one or a group effort—but couldn't recall ever having felt so alive doing it. She realized that almost all of the other times she had been pissed drunk. Most of her conquests were found at bars, and rarely culminated till late at night after marathon drinking sessions. The men would always climax prematurely, unless so drunk they were unable to perform. She would rarely achieve satisfaction, whether too numb from the alcohol, not primed before entry, or simply deprived of gratification due to her partner's hasty ejaculation. She preferred to be taken by a group of men, her theory being the more shooters, the better the chance of scoring a hit. Nonetheless, her choice of mates were more concerned with getting their jollies quickly so they'd make it back to their wives before sunrise. This would leave her to finish the job herself.

This occasion was different; both were sober, Hank Sr. was humping her as if he had just been recently released from prison, and she was wetter than she could remember ever being. Her thoughts were interrupted by a first Herculean climax.

Hank Sr. continued humping Jackie relentlessly; he had been celibate for far too long, to the point where he had even stopped thinking of women and sex. He had become comfortable with his monastic lifestyle. He rarely craved or wanted a woman, but when Jackie was making him breakfast that morning he had suddenly felt a flush of desire. He had surprised himself earlier when he took her in the stairwell; he was even more astonished when she allowed herself to be taken. He couldn't believe he was actually between the welcoming, open thighs of an exciting, sensual woman like her, twenty years his junior to boot. She writhed beneath him, her head thrown wildly from side to side as she received reward after reward.

Jackie lost all perception of time or space as orgasm after orgasm washed over her. Hank struggled to maintain his momentum while she thrashed about under him. Later, both lay side by side, sweaty, panting, with Hank sporting battle scars over his neck, shoulders and back. His member was finally spent. He couldn't recall his last erection, or its lasting so long. Jackie expressed her gratitude.

"Thank you, sir," she panted.

"No . . . thank YOU, Miss," he replied between shallow breaths.

Chapter 10

Saturday 8:15 a.m.

Jackie was awakened by a desperate urge to pee. The slightest movement made her feel as though her bladder would rupture. Grimacing in discomfort, she slowly swung her legs off the bed. She sat on the edge of the creaking mattress, pausing momentarily to allow her head time to accustom itself to the vertical position. She squinted at the small amount of light entering the room from around the drawn blinds. With a purposeful effort, she eventually hoisted herself to her feet, wavering a moment before heading for the washroom. She would normally awaken during the night to pee, but this time she'd slept right through from sheer physical exhaustion. Naked and unsteady, she waddled along with one hand cradling her lower abdomen while the other searched out furniture, walls, and doorframes basically anything that would steady her precarious walk to the toilet situated two doors down.

Once there, she plopped down wearily onto the toilet seat, and immediately her bladder started emptying. Cocking her head sideways, she let out a sigh of relief and she listened to the strong, seemingly interminable stream of urine filling the bowl. Her relief from voiding far surpassed the burning sensation coming from her abused vagina. Before long the stream became a trickle, and finally stopped. She sat quietly for some time, almost falling asleep again till her shoulder contacted the cool ceramic, jolting her awake. Slowly and still unsteadily, she arose, her eyes like slits. She automatically flushed the toilet before leaving the washroom. Drowsily she walked back to the bedroom, her shoulder intermittently rubbing up against the walls.

She let herself fall heavily onto the bed. The old springs sagged and creaked under her weight. When the bouncy mattress fell silent, she lay staring at the yellowing ceiling. Never had she ever been fucked so long and so hard. Young, athletic, big, strong, dexterous, she'd had them all; but none had come even remotely close to ravaging her in the way she'd been this time.

Hank Sr. turned to her; affectionately he nuzzled her ear, "Breakfast?" he offered.

When their flight landed they had grabbed a quick bite at the airport before being driven to a modest hotel by cab. Accommodations for the night were irrelevant, since their short stay only served as a diversion before they flew out again under their new identities. Marion saw the hotel manager slip the driver some money while they were signing in; obviously he was being paid a nominal royalty for bringing customers here. Once in their small room they disrobed, promptly falling asleep in each other's arms, exhaustion overruling any plans for passion.

Before Marion shook Martha awake, he'd been busy locating and booking a flight out to hopefully their final destination. Unable to find a direct commercial flight he'd chartered a flight. They would be leaving soon; he was glad they had both slept long and deep. Martha awoke; gently she smiled at her man and stretched. She put her arms around his shoulders and pulled him to her. "We've got to hustle, Martha," Marion told her.

"Just a short one, Honey," she teased.

Marion smiled, removing her arms from around his neck. "I know— but we're almost home free. Hang on just a little bit longer. For now we've got to go."

Martha pouted girlishly, cupping his groin she warned, "Once we get there you'll have to fulfill your promise."

Once dressed, they put their things in order. Martha Kowalski and Marion Lloyd, with a rip and a toss, were no more. They pillaged their wallets in order to remove all traces of their true identities, and replaced them with the false documentation they had acquired before leaving home. Martha took great pleasure in ripping up all her IDs. Marion noted she displayed a distinct purposefulness in her shredding of her old persona.

The taxi made its way to the busy international airport, bypassing the main terminal. Once there, they found the small air charter company that would fly them to their final destination. With their new identities they boarded the Lear jet for their final trek.

Saturday 10:32 a.m.

Another glorious summer day had arisen; dew still coated the lush grass of the cemetery grounds. A gentle breeze rustled the greenery. The only sounds were of birds chirping, traffic whizzing by on the nearby interstate, and the rumbling of a backhoe filling a grave a few rows down. The undeniable atmosphere of "life goes on" was tangible. As a fellow human was being put to rest, the world continued on its way, unimpeded.

Jackie and Hank Sr. stood by the gravesite holding hands. Both appeared sombre, but not distraught. Under different circumstances both would have given the impression of nonchalance. They politely listened to the preacher who ministered the appropriate rites; then a lone attendant activated the mechanism that lowered Hank Jr.'s casket into the welcoming earth. Both father and friend displayed no emotion at the sight of a son to one and lover to another disappearing into the ground. Hank Sr. bent over to scoop a handful of earth and threw it onto the casket. He shook his head solemnly, and Jackie wrapped her arm around his before they turned and left. Neither looked back once they began walking away. Hank Jr. was laid to rest next to his mother as he had lived, without recognition or fanfare.

Wincott sat in his office, a perplexed look on his face. He was trying to elicit interest in pursuing the Kowalski case. After having been exposed to the participants of this now unfortunate predicament, he had little interest in helping his client in the quest for a woman who, for all intents and purposes, seemed to have earned her freedom. But it was a job—and a potentially paying one at that. Besides, he had done much of the legwork already, and even had his quarry at arms length; so why not follow through? He assumed and was pretty certain that the two would take the money and run. Maybe move to another province, another country, or even another continent. Either way, he'd find them. The more he sat back to think about it, the more the chase instinct took over. Before long he was focused, and he picked up the phone to dial out.

The jet taxied to the small airport terminal, the doorway to their freedom. Andrew Robert Finley, a.k.a. Marion Lloyd, and Margaret Ann Bellini, a.k.a. Martha Kowalski, arrived at what they hoped was their final destination. Their new identities had served them well. The various airport security and immigration officials were none the wiser; the quality of the false documentation proved excellent and was well worth the money they had paid.

The chartered jet stopped near the terminal, its engines powering down. Soon the hatch opened, and the hot, humid tropical air struck them like the heat from a blast furnace. Martha had never experienced or felt such atmospheric intensity; she reached into her handbag to retrieve her sunglasses, the outside looked so bright under the sun of this hemisphere.

As they descended the short steps of the aircraft, a driver waved at them. Marion acknowledged him with a wave. The man politely opened the rear door and bowed to Martha as she took her place in the back seat. Thankfully it was air-conditioned; she took a deep breath of the refreshingly cool air before looking out to check on Marion. He was speaking to someone who was in uniform; it appeared to be an official of some sort. They stood on the hot tarmac speaking and passing some papers.

Marion felt nervous as the customs agent suspiciously scrutinized the documents he had handed him. Thankfully the sweat on his brow could easily be blamed on the heat. They had an eleven o'clock appointment with one of the many international banks situated on the island and Marion had no intention of missing it. As they were speaking, a white sedan pulled up, honking, with a distinguished-looking black gentleman at the wheel. He stopped a few feet from them, and, stepping out of the car, made his way towards them. He looked out of place in his tie and three-piece suit in the hot climate. He appeared to know the customs agent personally; amicably he shook the man's hand. Both appeared comfortable with each other. After having exchanged greetings, the man beamed a wide toothy smile in Marion's direction.

Hidden from Marion's view but within Martha's, the gentleman discreetly slipped an envelope to the customs agent. Martha then saw the newly arrived man shaking Marion's hand with vigour. They spoke amicably for some time before both finally walked over to the car where Martha was seated, and Marion introduced Jacques Dutellier as the bank's local administrator. He took her hand, kissing it.

Chapter 11

In the small town's main hotel, where Jacques had suggested they stay, Martha slept soundly. She had awakened from a deep, undisturbed slumber that had been more like a coma than anything else. The past couple of days of travel had exhausted her. She had been running on adrenaline till the previous night; she'd not felt the fatigue before then, but she now finally felt a sense of release. Marion lay still asleep. His deep, regular breathing indicated a profound sleep; he, too must have felt the same stress.

Propped up on one elbow, she stared at him, lying on his back, his taut chest rhythmically rising and falling with each breath. He appeared so calm; throughout the past week he'd been a rock for her. As complicated and hectic as things had been, he had remained a source of strength. She had gone through seemingly every emotion during that time, but he had remained stoic, confident, and logical. She would have committed many errors had it not been for his support and guidance, and this endeared him to her. She leaned forward, delicately kissing his forehead, careful not to awaken him.

Carefully she peeled back the bed sheet, slowly sliding her legs out to sit on the edge of the bed they shared. The golden light beginning to filter into the room indicated a glorious sunrise. Martha reached for her wristwatch resting on the bedside: 5:48 a.m. She slipped the Timex's band over her wrist and fastened the patent leather strap. She walked over to the dual curtain-draped French doors opening onto the modest wrought iron railing balcony. Squinting at the bright onslaught of the rising sun, she stepped onto the gallery. The day's impending heat was already palpable.

From her third-floor perch she could see a vast field of growing produce. She couldn't tell what the waist-high plants were; all she could discern in the distance was a group of labourers making their way down a path towards the lush field. The dozen or so farm workers, men and women of various ages, carrying shovels, scythes, rakes, and baskets, slowly made their way down a small hill. On the horizon her view was impeded by a low-lying mist she assumed must be the ocean. She'd seen the ocean for the first time the day before from the airplane. She hoped the day's tasks would allow them to go and see the coast. She closed her eyes for a moment and breathed in the clean air before pulling up a plastic patio chair and sitting down.

The phone rang on the night table next to Marion. It was a black phone with a rotary dial—surely it hailed back to the 1950s. Its ringer was annoyingly loud; he reached over to pick up. The receiver was heavy in his hand; misjudging its weight, he slammed it hard against his temple. Annoyed, he answered, "Yes, what is it!"

"Signor, it is eight o'clock, your wake-up call," a tinny voice informed him.

"Thank you," he replied before replacing the receiver.

Rubbing his eyes with closed fists, he yawned before opening them. Squinting at the bright sunlit room, he noted the air was already heavy and humid, prompting him to question the effectiveness of the air conditioning. Glancing to his right, he noted Martha's absence.

"Martha, MARTHA!" he called.

Jumping to his feet, he rushed to the washroom, which was empty. He jerked open the door to the hall, startling a maid with his abruptness. Apologizing, he closed the door. His heart raced till he noted a figure on the balcony slumped in a chair, her feet up against the railing. Clad only in a long T-shirt and panties. He stepped out and kneeled down on one knee, noting with relief that she was asleep. He gently kissed her shoulder, moist from perspiration. Martha lifted her head, dazed by his touch; she turned her head and smiled at him.

"Marion, it's so beautiful here," she commented.

Kissing her lips, he nodded his agreement.

Oscar Garcia found his potential clients breakfasting in the hotel's dining room. He immediately noted their youth. He strode towards them with his hand out.

"Mr. and Mrs. Finley?" he politely asked.

Marion rose to shake his hand, "Yes. Mr. Garcia?"

"It is nice to meet you," replied Garcia.

Marion, pulling out a chair, invited him to sit.

He greeted Martha with a handshake and a smile. "I am sent by Jacques. He informed me that you are looking for a home," he confirmed before sitting.

Oscar Garcia felt immediately at ease with his new prospects. They appeared perfectly matched, although younger than his normal clientele for this kind of real estate. Jacques had informed him of the type of home and price range they were interested in. Had not Jacques informed him beforehand of their ability to afford an expensive home, he would have immediately concluded by their appearance that they were far less wealthy. He'd brought several listings with him in his worn cowhide briefcase he'd received as a gift from his now deceased parents thirty years earlier when he entered the domain of real estate. He could now afford a newer document carrier than the heavy, tattered one he had, but his father had made it from thick shoe leather when he was a cobbler. It had sentimental value.

He proceeded to confirm what Jacques had told him: that they wanted a furnished property they could move into immediately. Marion, in turn, confirmed they were interested only in renting at this time with an option to buy, if the owner wished to do so. Oscar pulled three listings from his bag he'd pre-selected. Marion put up his hand, interrupting the task of spreading documents on the table.

"My wife and I are both very visual people—we'd much prefer to see the properties. Although our night here was very comfortable, we'd like very much to visit and decide on this today."

"Very well, Señor, if you like we can drive to see them this morning." Both Marion and Martha nodded in agreement.

The three of them walked out towards Oscar's car, an older American model. It was clean and well maintained, parked down the street from their hotel. Martha sat in the back seat while Marion sat in front next to Oscar.

"I will show you three houses which may interest you; we'll start with the closest."

During the drive, Marion sat with his arm over the back of his seat, casually chatting with Martha and Oscar. After a short distance, Oscar turned off the main road, which had meandered through farmland, onto an unmarked gravel road bordered by dense brush. A couple of hundred yards later, the narrow path cleared, and a two-storey Victorian-style house came into view. Martha leaned forward in her seat, impressed by the home.

"Wow, it's beautiful!" she exclaimed.

Marion seemed less impressed. They exited the cool confines of the car to gaze at the house. Martha seemed caught in a trance as she stepped onto the canopied wood porch surrounding the large house. Thick ornamental wood posts spaced at eight-foot intervals supported the shingled porch roof. Martha looked in awe at the impressive structure. Gardens surrounded the property bordered by dense vegetation and trees. Oscar was detailing the property's information, while Marion stood surveying the grounds with his arms crossed.

"Too isolated," he commented.

Martha turned to look at him, stunned by his comment.

"What? It's gorgeous! Let's see the inside, at least."

"If you want, Honey, but it's too removed," he pointed out.

"This whole island is removed—isn't that the point?" she asked.

"Yes, but we can do better. Right, Mr. Garcia?" he asked, turning to their guide.

"I suppose—it depends what you wish for," Oscar replied. "I have two more properties to show you; shall we go?" he asked.

"Yes, let's do that," Marion confirmed, slipping his arm around Martha's shoulders.

Shortly after they had pulled back onto the main road, they found themselves driving along the coast. Martha let out an audible gasp when the ocean came into view. Marion turned to see her girlish expression of delight at what she saw. He beamed a wide smile when he saw her excitement. Martha was awed by the azure blue seascape, dotted with greenish patches from the coral reefs. She pressed her hand against the window, marvelling at the natural beauty of the palm trees, the vast expanse of beach, the almost neon-blue water.

"Marion, my God, it's so . . . beautiful!" she expressed with wonder. "These places really do exist!"

"Yes, they do," he confirmed. "Welcome to your new home, Honey."

Martha lifted her hand to her open mouth, still marvelling at the glorious view. Shortly after, Oscar turned off the road once again, and drove up a rise and down a winding two-lane paved road.

"The other two homes are situated in a coastal community; I believe it will be more what you wish for," Oscar commented.

Marion simply nodded in confirmation. The road led up to a barrier next to a twelve-foot-square guardhouse. Chickens and a goat milled about the modest cabin. A uniformed man came out of the house to greet them. The man smiled at Oscar and approached to shake his hand. Courteous conversation was exchanged between the two men. The stocky guard stepped inside; he could be seen picking up a phone to dial, then stepping back out to lift the wooden barrier to let them drive in. The narrow road made its way up an incline that was lined with statuesque palm trees, and in the distance scattered homes of various architectural designs and sizes could be seen. Oscar pulled up in front of the first, a single-storey ranch house close to the road.

"This is another house—"

"No," Marion interrupted.

Bowing to his wishes, Oscar pulled away.

"The next one, I am certain, will be to your liking, Señor," he stated, accelerating away.

Within minutes after driving along the winding road and passing a half-dozen more homes, he pulled into a stone driveway framed by tall bushes. Around a bend, a two-storey house came into view. White, grand, pillars lined its façade, and it was crowned by a red tile roof. It exuded old-world Spanish architecture. One of the double mahogany front doors opened to reveal a bearded, tall, slim, older gentleman in a dark suit. He stood at the ready when they stopped to exit the car. Behind them stood a short, stocky woman wearing a maid's uniform, her hands clasped at her chest. Oscar invited Marion and Martha to come up the granite steps to the house.

Marion, taking Martha's hand, accepted his invitation.

"This is more like it," he commented to Martha.

Following his lead, all she could manage was a subtle nod; her awe was evident. Oscar introduced the staff as Carlos and Susanna. They were informed that Carlos was the butler; he handled all the administration of the house. Susanna fulfilled the function of maid and cook. When they stepped into the foyer he explained that the owners were an American businessman and his wife. The reason the house was on the market was that the owner had recently accepted a position as CEO in a high-profile company, and since his responsibilities required him to establish himself in Europe, he had little time for his villa on the island. As such he wished to sell it, or, at the very least, rent it out.

While he spoke, Martha and Marion admired the house's design. Oscar noted their obvious interest and invited them to visit the house. He started by leading them up the grand stairway to the second floor, where they found a spacious parlour giving an appreciable view of the grounds at the back of the mansion. From there they had a view of the terraced gardens leading down to the ocean.

Facing the stairs was the master bedroom, situated at the front of the house. The suite was a vast expanse, featuring a large Jacuzzi and private bath, fireplace, and lounging area. The room was bright, with several floor-to-ceiling windows. Two wide French doors led to the large veranda facing the front of the house. They were both very impressed with the accommodations. The entire house was tastefully furnished with dark wood furniture.

Once back downstairs, they were shown the living room, kitchen, and dining room, which bordered a paved and landscaped courtyard whose centrepiece was an enormous abstract in-ground pool sporting a concrete island with a waterfall, being tended to by a shirtless young man retrieving leaves with a pole and net. All was extraordinarily impressive. Both Martha and Marion were speechless throughout the guided tour of the manor.

Oscar walked them through the grounds, pointing out the various features of the property: the two-car garage, the pool house, manicured gardens, and direct access to the beach. Once back inside, all three sat at the dining room table to discuss the conditions and terms of renting the luxurious property.

In island terms, the monthly price was extravagant; however, in North American terms it was quite reasonable, considering the value of the estate. A condition was, however, stipulated that the longstanding staff be kept on. The owner felt a strong devotion towards the loyal employees. Marion and Martha were more than willing to accept the suitable request; they would need a staff to administer the household anyhow. Marion asked for a moment with his wife. Oscar rose to oblige the request. Marion invited him to remain seated; he and his new mate would discuss the matter while strolling the grounds.

Both walked out to the back of the house.

"Well?" Marion asked.

"Well what? My God, it's magnificent! What do *you* think?" Martha asked.

"The price seems right," he commented.

"I know! How can it be?"

"Well, if you consider the island's standards and economy, it seems a valid price. And the staff would only cost us a few hundred more a month. I'm sure the owner doesn't care to keep it empty during his absence; besides, according to the agent, his ultimate goal is to sell the property to any potential renter."

Martha nodded in agreement just as they reached the end of the winding path leading down to the beach. Awe struck her once again. Even Marion took a deep breath at the glorious view. A gentle breeze rustled the abundant foliage behind them, along with the palm trees dotting the sandy private shoreline.

"Let's do it. There's no harm in signing for a year, I suppose. What do you think?" she again asked.

Martha was unsure if Marion was pondering the question or staring fixedly at the ocean in a state of astonishment. She squeezed his hand to elicit a response, and he turned to her, taking her in his arms.

"Let's do it," he simply said before deeply embracing her.

Oscar sat quietly at the table. Carlos stood next to him, pouring him another cup of coffee while clearing the plates speckled with cake crumbs from the table. Oscar calmly contemplated the gardens through the dining room's glass wall. He had a feeling the deal would go through. His years of experience told him his two potential clients—especially Marion—seemed to know what they wanted. Marion had been quick to discount the first two properties, while this one seemed to appeal to the couple immediately. Finally he saw them returning hand in hand back up the path. He smiled to himself. From their demeanour he could tell they'd made a decision—a positive one.

Upon entering the room, Marion nudged Martha, who with a wide smile informed Oscar, "We'll take it."

"All the terms are acceptable, Señora?" he questioned.

"Yes, of course," Martha assured him.

Carlos nodded in Susanna's direction. She smiled a smile of relief before crossing herself and leaving for the kitchen.

"How soon can we move in?" Martha inquired.

Oscar, displaying an expression of nonchalance, replied, "Once the papers are signed, immediately. I have the papers in the car; this can be resolved today, if you wish."

"Yes, I'd . . . we'd like that very much, Mr. Garcia."

Oscar rose to retrieve his briefcase from the car. Martha and Marion hugged and kissed, both very happy with their decision to establish themselves here. Before long Oscar had returned with the required paperwork. The new owners heard Oscar conversing with Carlos and Susanna. Upon entering the room, Susanna swiftly ran to Martha, eagerly hugging her. She rambled on excitedly in Spanish. All Martha could do in return was shrug her shoulders and smile. She couldn't understand a word the maid was saying.

Chapter 12

Martha quickly adapted to her new life. After a week on the island she had only a distant memory of her life up to this point. Whenever she recalled how she'd arrived at this stage, it seemed to her that she was thinking of someone else. She was far more self-assured now; the years of abuse that had destroyed her confidence and dampened her intelligence were a part of the distant past— that was another person.

She had, however, retained her helpful attitude; she chuckled to herself when she recalled the first night at her new home when she'd stepped into the kitchen to bring Susanna the dinner plates to wash. The maid had greeted her with wide-eyed astonishment, quickly taking the dishes from her and rambling on about her not inconveniencing herself with tasks. She recalled when she'd returned to the dining room; Marion sat with wine glass in hand, chuckling,

"You asked for it!"

After that she conceded to the maid's determination, allowing herself to be pampered.

Sitting in the shade next to the pool, she casually observed Lisle, the groundskeeper, as he went about his chores. He was spreading some cedar bark around the flowerbeds that dotted the property. She sipped her lemonade from a tall glass, sweating dew on her palm. After a week she only knew the young man's name as Lisle. She'd see him here and there, mostly in the distance doing his work, mowing the lawn, tending the grounds, and maintaining the house. He obviously had the lowest of the positions within the household. The only contact she'd had in his regard was a nod or a wave of acknowledgement.

Her thoughts soon returned to her undertaking of learning to speak Spanish. Jacques from the bank had suggested the best way to start was reading the local Spanish paper, with a Spanish/English dictionary to decipher the text. She found this method laborious, and after a week could recognize quite a few words but still could not formulate sentences. Her concentration was interrupted by a loud clank, making her drop her glass onto the paving stones.

Lisle ran to her, apologizing profusely: his shovel had slipped off the rim of the wheelbarrow and fallen loudly onto the pavement.

"I'm sorry, Madam. Are you all right? I'll clean this up immediately," he assured her.

"You speak English," she commented.

His head stooped, concentrating on picking up the shards of glass, he confirmed, "Yes, Madam, I do."

"You speak it very well."

"Thank you, Madam. I'll be right back; please don't put your bare feet down till I pick up all the broken glass," he cautioned before scurrying off to the maintenance shed to retrieve a broom and dustpan. While he was away, Martha had an idea. Upon Lisle's return to clean up the mess, she proposed an arrangement.

"Lisle, since you are fluent in both English and Spanish, would you mind setting aside an hour or so a day to teach me?"

Lisle contemplated the question without looking up from his chore. Finally he answered without looking up, "I don't think Mr. Carlos would appreciate me socializing with the lady of the house."

"Why? Is it a problem?" she asked, perplexed.

Just then Carlos came out of the house, when he saw Lisle down on one knee conversing with the Lady of the House, he reacted angrily.

"*¿Qué haces? ¡Vuelve a trabajar!*" he snapped.

Martha quickly grabbed Lisle's arm when he stood to leave. "Wait! Explain to Carlos," she demanded.

With downcast eyes, Lisle turned and said to Carlos, "*La señora desea que le enseñe español.*"

With raised eyebrows Carlos replied in surprise, "*¿Usted? ¿Dónde obtuvo ella esa idea loca?*"

Lisle shrugged his shoulders; Martha rose to defend him.

"Carlos, he speaks both languages. I'd like him to teach me, just an hour a day."

Squinting, Carlos turned his head in an attempt to better understand her. Lisle translated her request: "*La señora desea que le ayude a aprender el español, por una hora al día.*"

Carlos, raising his eyebrows in surprise and looking back and forth between Martha and Lisle, finally spoke. "*No es apropiado. Pero si eso es lo que ella desea,*" he said, shrugging his shoulders.

Just then Marion ran up the path from the beach, returning from his morning jog. "What's wrong?" he inquired between pants.

"Nothing, Honey. Lisle here, speaks very fluent English. I'd like him to teach me Spanish," Martha clarified.

Both Lisle and Carlos stood looking very uncomfortable.

"Really?" Marion commented. "That sounds fine to me; go ahead. I'm going to take a shower." He turned and jogged his way towards the house.

Carlos bowed before taking his leave, but not before glaring in Lisle's direction.

"That settles that. We'll start this afternoon," Martha adamantly confirmed.

Lisle nodded in affirmation before turning to get back to work. He felt very uncomfortable about the arrangement; it felt especially disconcerting since the mistress was so young and beautiful. He knew full well Carlos would continue being in opposition to the arrangement.

Jacques pulled into the car dealership's lot with Marion and Martha as passengers. The dealership was one of the only ones on the small island; Jacques had offered to accompany the young couple he'd seemingly graciously taken under his wing since their arrival, so they could order a car for themselves. Once inside, Jacques introduced them to the sales manager. Martha wished for a sensible, comfortable vehicle while Marion leaned towards a sportier means of transportation. The small showroom contained only three vehicles, all of which were powerful European sedans. One immediately caught Maratha's eye; she walked over to it while Marion spoke to the salesman. It was a black Volkswagen Passatt.

She walked past the blue BMW 3 series sedan and a copper-coloured Volvo S60 without giving them a second glance. She walked around the Passatt, gently stroking the automobile's fluid lines with the fingertips of one hand, occasionally bending down to look inside at the grey leather interior. She was truly impressed. Sliding in on the driver's seat, she looked over at Marion, flashing a look of admiration for the car.

Marion, viewing a binder, smiled back at her, and teasingly said, "Always the consummate conservative."

"It's beautiful, look!" she replied.

Taking the binder, he walked over to her, leaning into the car, his forearms resting atop the driver's door. He gave the interior a glance.

"Yes, it is nice, but not for us."

Martha gasped at his comment. "Why not?"

Smiling, he stood up, and turned the binder towards her, showing the page he'd been looking at. Her eyes opened wide.

"You're kidding, right?"

Smiling, he shook his head. "This one is *you*."

He propped up the catalogue in her lap, leaning it against the Passat's leather-clad steering wheel, his forefinger pointing out his suggestion.

"My God, Marion!"

"Honey, no kids yet, the world is at our feet—so why not?"

Looking at the picture, she contemplated his choice: a Porsche 911 Turbo. Even in the photograph it seemed to pounce at her.

"It is beautiful, but . . ."

"But?" he repeated.

"Is it . . . practical?" she questioned.

Marion laughed wholeheartedly. "Practical? Who cares? Do you like it?"

Martha stared at the cover for a moment before flipping through the pages; she admired the interior, its sensual lines, and its low, assertive stance. Glancing once more at the Volkswagen's interior, it suddenly had as much appeal as sensible shoes.

"What colour?" was all she could venture to say.

Over the next few weeks, Martha continued to adapt well to her new environment. Most of her days revolved around a habitual routine. They'd rise at around eight or nine in the morning, dress, and then go down for breakfast out in the pool area. Most days were rain free; it rained mostly in the late evenings or overnight. By morning, lingering clouds would make way for bright sunshine and hot temperatures. Marion would read the paper, mainly the *New York Times*, which was flown in daily from the mainland for the many foreign residents. After an unhurried breakfast, they would usually make their way down the winding path to the beach, where they would swim and lounge in the sun till lunch. Two-way radios would allow them to communicate with their staff if they required anything.

Their secluded oasis permitted them to indulge in clandestine activities such as swimming in the nude or passionate lovemaking in their natural surroundings. Sex had become a welcome daily pastime for Martha and her mate. An activity that had been loathsome to her during her pitiful marriage was now a welcome interlude in her new life. Marion was a considerate, capable lover and she cherished being able to please him at every opportunity. Their pleasant routine would continue at midday where, depending on their mood, they would either take a light lunch, served on the beach, or be served a more substantial meal on the terrace by the pool and gardens.

In the afternoon Martha's time would be her own. Marion would usually take a cab or get a lift into town to meet with local or foreign business people whom Jacques had introduced to him in order to discuss various business opportunities. However, most days upon his return he'd relate how he'd spent the last few hours—golfing, deep sea fishing, or simply socializing with his new friends and acquaintances. This suited Martha fine, since the few times she'd accompanied Marion she'd inevitably end up having tea or shopping with the wives and companions of his acquaintances. She'd end up feeling patronized by the well-to-do women and was quickly introduced to the demeaning term of "*nouveau riche*." She much preferred to spend the afternoons studying Spanish with Lisle.

Lisle had become a welcome companion, kind, considerate, and pleasant to be with. She was learning her new language by leaps and bounds. They would converse in Spanish for hours at a time. This served the purpose of not only allowing her to practise the language, but also to learn about life in the tropics from Lisle. This served a therapeutic purpose as well, since she would then relate her previous life to him. Lisle in turn appreciated Martha's refreshing down-to-earth personality, so rarely seen in outsiders. Contrary to the island's mores and way of life, he had developed a sincere liking for his employer. Martha as well found herself captivated by the young man. Both were very conscious of how inappropriately their friendship was viewed by the other staff. For this reason they conducted their lessons well within view.

Chapter 13

One month later . . .

Another glorious day, hot, sunny with a slight breeze blowing inland from the coast. It brought with it the smell of the ocean, but no relief from the stifling heat. Already at 9:30 in the morning the heat was intense. The road's blacktop absorbed and in turn radiated the torridity. The air-conditioned car insulated Jacques from the outside blaze. Locals went about their business seemingly immune to the inferno. Along the road, he passed children playing, women carrying bundles, and men on bikes, as well as the occasional elderly man sitting in fortuitous spots of shade.

Jacques Dutellier had become a close friend and confidant to the island's new arrivals. Strangers to the local culture, they were inexperienced in the ways of the people, traditions, laws, and their own newfound wealth. Turning off the main road, he arrived at the guardhouse isolating the exclusive gated community from the island's poverty. In it sat the uniformed sentinel who leapt to his feet when he spotted the approaching car. The black man politely asked Jacques whom he was visiting in order to confirm his arrival. Once confirmation by telephone of his expected arrival was verified and consented to, access was granted and the man stepped into the sun to manually raise the wooden barrier. Jacques drove in, nodding a thank you.

He steered his car along the winding, scenic road leading up to the home of his newfound friends and valued customers. Carlos stood wearing slacks, shirt, and bow tie on the porch, hands clasped before him. Jacques parked in the shade of a large tree, and then stepped out of his car. He dabbed sweat from his forehead with a handkerchief during the short walk to the grandiose, mahogany double front doors. The butler nodded and informed Jacques that the Masters were dining on the terrace next to the pool.

Jacques stepped into the house, taking a welcome breath of the cool air inside. Momentarily he checked himself in the mirror hanging in the vast entrance, taking the time to straighten his stripped tie before proceeding to the back. He spotted his hosts through the windowed patio door leading to the pool area. He could see them on the far side of the pool on the stone terrace overlooking the ocean. Upon sliding the door open, he was relieved to feel a refreshing breeze rising up the hill from the beach below. Marion, who was facing him, rose to his feet, smiling; Martha turned to greet their visitor as well.

Heartily he shook Marion's hand before taking Martha's hand and kissing it. Martha blushed at his chivalrous greeting. He had brought by some paperwork to be signed. The new island residents had adopted Jacques as a friend and confidant. Through his numerous other involvements, he was wise to the financial world and local politics. He was apt at navigating the various channels for the newly arrived millionaires. Marion and Martha trusted him; he had proven a worthy ally in their quest for acceptance into the local community. Jacques cared for them as well; but after all, business is business . . .

Wincott wished he could avoid this meeting, but as a client Hank Sr. was entitled to an update even if it was not a positive one. Wincott was to tell them that his investigation into the whereabouts of Martha Kowalski had led to a dead end. He'd known this pretty well a good three weeks ago, but hung onto the hope that something would develop and he would pick up a scent. Unfortunately that was not to be; and upon the insistence or Hank Sr. he was going to have to inform him of what little he had so far.

Hank Sr. entered Wincott's office, holding hands with Jackie. Wincott hadn't seen him in weeks. He looked good; his attire was not dated, like the last time he'd seen him. Pleated khaki pants, indigo blue Polo, open-toed walking sandals, with matching belt. He looked ten years younger. Even Jackie was different, her clothing, although still quite revealing and tight fitting, was less . . . "sluttish." He judged she had dropped a good ten pounds. She wore a just-above-the-knee form-fitting jean dress, with buttons all down the front—the top three unbuttoned. Her platinum blonde hair had given way to a flattering subdued brunette colour, streaked with blondish highlights. Even her makeup was more reserved; gone were the loud facial colours. Her full lips were a darker shade of red, her eyes highlighted with mascara; gone were the purple eye shadow and red cheekbones. Wincott commented to himself he would take notice of her in a crowded room.

Jackie sat down first; tugging down her skirt and nodding a greeting, she crossed her legs. This time he would not have to view her opened thighs as he was forced to do the last time she sat in his office. Hank Sr. sat down on the chair next to her; he, too, nodded a greeting, but didn't reach over the desk to shake Wincott's hand. Hank Sr. crossed his legs, and, with hands resting on his lap, waited for the other to speak. Uncomfortably, Wincott began.

Juanita Mendoza, a stunningly beautiful mulatto woman, applied her makeup in her modest apartment. Born in South America, she had lost her mother at a very young age. Since then she'd accompanied her father all over South America, the Caribbean, and anywhere else he could find work as a mineral expert in the mining industry. She earned her living in a combination of ways: as an assistant to Jacques Dutellier, and as a tourist guide on weekends. Mainly, she rounded out her months by servicing rich residents and tourists as an escort. Almost all her contacts came through Jacques; he was essentially her pimp, for lack of a better word.

Recently Jacques had discussed with her the newest arrivals on the island, Andrew Finley and his wife, Margaret. Although Jacques was well paid as far as island standards went, he had a prominent greedy streak. Somehow no amount of money was enough for him; he resented the rich foreigners who migrated here to live out their fantasy lives in the tax haven that was his country. A combination of almost no tax exposure and a very low cost of living made this country a true tropical paradise for them.

Most of the economy stemmed from tourism and catering to the numerous millionaires who called the island home. Jacques quickly determined that Finley and his wife were not from "old money." How they had acquired their wealth was a mystery to Jacques. He was not privy to the information, or how long they had been married or been together. All Jacques knew was they had arrived with a large sum of money. Finley had experience in law, and his pretty wife was sweet but very naïve. Jacques was quick to note Finley's weak points to be pretty women and gambling—both of which Jacques had every intention of exploiting, with Juanita's help.

Under the pretext of aiding them to get established and familiarized with their new environment, as well as to gain their trust, Jacques had graciously escorted the recent arrivals around. He had helped them acquire staff and servants, as well as introducing them to the local hotspots. He had noted Andrew's eyes lighting up when they had driven by the island's casino, and he seemed very interested, even anxious, to visit it. Jacques had made arrangements so he could take him there under the pretext of a boy's night out; and tonight was that night.

Jackie and Hank Sr. declined the offer of coffee. Hank Sr. squirmed uncomfortably in his seat. Wincott acknowledged their anxiousness and swallowed before beginning.

"My investigation has come to an unfortunate dead end. Credit card transactions, sightings, traceable movements all ceased suddenly about four weeks ago."

Jackie turned to glimpse Hank's reaction, but Hank Sr. continued staring back at Wincott blankly.

Wincott continued, "Besides tracing your daughter-in-law's few possessions to a storage unit across town, I've been at a loss to find any other trace of her or of her lawyer, whom I strongly believe she's built a bond and very likely a relationship with. I suspect they've likely moved to another province, in which case their whereabouts will surely resurface. They could have left the country; however, neither possesses a valid passport, nor have they applied for one. At this point I'm relying on information coming my way. At some point in time they will surely resurface."

Hank Sr. stirred uncomfortably in his seat; he seemed to be battling fury or hemorrhoids. Both Wincott and Jackie looked his way for confirmation.

"So you've got dick," he finally said.

"I've got as much now for you as I had for your son. You must understand the difficulty of finding someone who doesn't want to be found." Wincott swallowed.

"So dick is all we're gonna have," Hank interjected.

"No . . . Dick is what we have now. It doesn't mean it's over. It means until new information surfaces, we'll have to wait."

Hank Sr. avoided Wincott's eyes. Nervously his eyes darted about the room.

"Listen, I'll remain on the case if you wish. Since what I've done for you is just to reconfirm what I already had for your son, payment will be postponed till a new lead is established. Okay?"

Hank Sr. reluctantly agreed. He stood, and without any eye contact shook Wincott's hand before shuffling out the door, obviously disappointed, if not angry. Jackie mimicked his every move after nodding and smiling at Wincott. Wincott had to admire Jackie's form, she looked good since the last time . . . Damn good.

Marion and Jacques stepped out of the cab and walked up the casino steps together, where a large-framed doorman opened the heavy brass and glass door for them. Marion couldn't help but think of the 90/10 rule: Outside the casino, ninety percent of the people were black, but inside, ninety percent were white. The ten percent seemed to be made up of black workers serving an almost exclusively white patronage. Jacques led him to the roulette table.

There, Jacques changed two hundred American dollars into chips and slid half over to Marion. "My weakness is roulette," Jacques confessed.

"I know the feeling," Marion replied under his breath, while anxiously taking in his surroundings. Marion felt ill at ease in the noisy casino environment; the bells, clanging, jingling of the machines was overwhelming. His attention was drawn to everything; he was experiencing sensory overload when Jacques tugged at his arm.

"Are you all right, Andrew?"

"Of course. Let's try our luck," he proposed to Jacques.

They both took a seat at a gaming table. Marion decided to start easy, and placed a ten-dollar chip on the black section of the game mat. Jacques placed twenty dollars on number two, red. The croupier, a slim, young black man, panned his hand over the table signifying no more bets before spinning the roulette wheel and tossing in the ball. Marion stared intently at the spinning wheel and ball. Finally the little sphere lost momentum, clashing with the wheel's raised ridges defining the numbered compartments. It bounced around for a moment before nestling into a numbered compartment.

The wheel slowed enough for Marion to see that the niche the ball had settled into was black. Jacques exclaimed, "Ah, merde! Eight black."

At that moment, his cellular rang. Feigning annoyance, Jacques answered it.

"Yes . . . yes . . . NOW? I'm afraid that's impossible, I am… Fine, I'll be there shortly." He flipped his phone closed, cursing.

Jacques turned to Marion. "I'm sorry, Andrew, we'll have to cut our evening short. A client has an administrative problem I must attend to immediately."

The croupier slid a ten-dollar chip towards Marion's bet. He let it ride.

"Of course, Jacques, I understand," Marion reassured him.

The croupier spun the wheel again.

Juanita Mendoza hung up the public phone in the entrance. She spotted Jacques from across the casino floor. She noted a rather attractive man sitting next to him at the gaming table. She had been informed by Jacques the intended target was young; looks were of little interest to her since she had concluded long ago that looks and money were a rare combination. She glided towards them; Jacques glanced her way before returning his attention to the spinning wheel. Juanita tapped Jacques' shoulder and he turned, feigning surprise.

"Ah, Juanita, what a surprise!"

Pulling Marion's attention from the game, he said, "Andrew, allow me to present you to Juanita, a dear friend and associate."

Marion turned towards Jacques; his expression did little to hide his awe at what he saw. He did a quick take of the vision before him, legs, waist, breasts, and, finally, her face. He took her hand, which was extended in a greeting. Clumsily he stood, almost tipping his stool. Juanita giggled sweetly.

"This is perfect, Andrew. I will leave you in Juanita's company. Juanita, do you mind?"

"Of course not. I was to meet a girlfriend of mine, but she cancelled unexpectedly."

"Andrew?"

"Of course, Jacques, you go ahead."

"Excellent, Andrew. I'm certain Juanita will take good care of you." With that he took his leave.

Marion invited Juanita to the bar for a drink. They strolled away from the table just as the croupier announced "16 red," and pulled Marion's money away.

Marion and Juanita sat and talked for hours. Marion seemed infatuated by the exotic beauty. Juanita herself enjoyed his company; she debated if anything sexual should take place that night. Her instinct dictated no, although her libido said yes; but she knew that whatever took place tonight would have to be initiated by him. Juanita glanced at her watch: it was 2:20 a.m.

Marion took the cue, "I'm sorry, it's late. Do you wish to go?" he asked politely.

"No . . . but I must," she replied sweetly. "Do you have a car?"

Marion flushed, "Um, no, I came with Jacques!"

"No problem, I will drive you."

"I don't want to be a bother—"

"Don't be silly. It'll be a chance to talk longer," she assured him.

Marion followed Juanita to her car, a modest two-door compact.

Martha couldn't sleep; she stared at the clock on her bedside table: almost three o'clock. She didn't expect Marion home early from his night out with Jacques, but didn't think it would be this late. She didn't mind him going out, but he'd never stayed out this late. Although she felt safe in the huge villa she was still conscious of the fact she was far from home. She disliked it when Marion wasn't with her. Martha opened the French doors that led to the bedroom balcony overlooking the long driveway up to the front of the house. She was relieved to see Marion walking up the drive and she called to him. He looked up and waved to her before entering downstairs.

Juanita drove along the secluded road leading back to town; she'd dropped off her new acquaintance at the gates to his villa. He explained that he wished to walk the short distance up the drive to his house, but she knew that he surely did not care to have his wife question him on his escort. She had stopped her car and even applied the handbrake in case he fancied an involved farewell; however, he offered a gentlemanly handshake with a kind good evening, even though she'd turned in her seat to face him, giving him a view of her enticing thighs. He did, however, glance at her provocative figure before taking his leave. She was confident she would have him soon enough.

Marion walked into the bedroom loosening his tie; Martha hugged him.

"Didn't Jacques dri—" Martha attempted to ask before Marion kissed her passionately.

Chapter 14

Martha looked at Marion suspiciously; he had breakfasted with her, and then promptly changed into slacks and a shirt. He claimed to have an appointment with Jacques in order to finalize a few things. She'd been growing suspicious of him lately. Before arriving on the island they'd been inseparable, planning and structuring their new life together. Since their arrival he'd been growing distant. Last night they'd made love for the first time in days, but it was different. Not unpleasant, just different.

He didn't as much make love to her as much as fucked her. It was far more ardent than usual, he took her in a way that she'd categorize as savage, and it was over within minutes. Last night, he had definitely come home horny.

Marion pecked her on the cheek and left when the taxi honked out front. They were still awaiting delivery of the car they'd ordered. Meanwhile, they received lifts from the staff or relied on cabs for transportation. As Marion was leaving, Lisle arrived. He cordially greeted her as Mrs. Margaret; she still wasn't used to her alias and often would reply in a delayed fashion. Of all the hired help she appreciated Lisle the most; he was polite, courteous, and always offered to be of assistance. In his early twenties, she considered him attractive as well, in a young, innocent sort of way.

Marion walked into Jacques' office. Juanita was standing dutifully next to Jacques, who was sitting at his desk. She held some papers and was waiting for Jacques to get off the phone. Jacques waved Marion in, inviting him to sit. His eyes met Juanita's. Both flashed a timid smile at one another.

Marion whispered, "You got home all right last night, Juanita?"

"Yes, thank you," she whispered back. "Did you sleep well?"

"Yes, but not long."

Jacques put down the phone and flashed his patented toothy grin. "Ola, Andrew, what brings you here, my friend?"

"Um, I dropped by to finalize the car payments we discussed," Marion answered.

"Car payments? For the Porsche? But I told you all was taken care of with the car dealership—your car should be here any day now," Jacques responded.

"Oh, yes, that's right, now I remember," Marion blushed. "Sorry."

"Not at all, my friend." Jacques glanced at his watch. "It's early for lunch."

Looking at Juanita, then back at Marion, he asked, "What time did you two get home last night?"

Juanita answered, "Oh, it was well past two."

Jacques turned to her, frowning. "TWO? My God, you two must be exhausted. Juanita, I will need you refreshed by tomorrow to work on that hotel development loan. Meanwhile, why don't you accompany my friend Andrew for a coffee and then go home and rest."

Juanita shrugged her shoulders, "I don't mind, Jacques, unless Andrew is busy?"

"NO, not at all!" Marion replied, rising to his feet.

"Excellent, off with the both of you then," Jacques ordered.

Marion and Juanita left the bank's offices and crossed the street to the small café. Before going in, Juanita billowed the blouse under her dark business suit, "Oof, it's hot," she declared, removing her jacket.

"Yes, it is," Marion agreed.

"Would you mind if I changed at my apartment?" she asked.

"Of course not. Do you live far?" Marion asked.

"No, just a couple of blocks from here. Come, it will only take a few minutes." Taking his hand, she led him up the street.

Once at her modest tenement, she invited Marion upstairs. Once there, she invited him to sit in the parlour while she changed. Juanita stepped into her room, not bothering to close the door. Marion could still see her through the reflection in a dressing table mirror across from him. Prudently he observed her peel her clothes off till she stood in only her panties. Bending over she retrieved a T-shirt and shorts from her dresser. Her fabulous breasts hung seductively from her chest while she rummaged through her drawers. She returned to him wearing her casual attire.

He couldn't help but admire her tight body clothed in the light garb. She offered him a drink, suggesting it was too hot for coffee. He readily accepted, and once again was treated to the sight of Juanita's buxom rump when she bent over to retrieve two beers from the fridge. She sat next to him on the couch with one leg bent, facing him while leaning against the sofa back. She handed him his beer, then took a long drink from her bottle. He seemed spellbound by her sensually long smooth throat that rhythmically contracted as she swallowed her cold brew. Lightheaded, he felt himself heedlessly leaning forward.

Juanita was surprised by his boldness when she felt his lips on her throat, and inadvertently she spilled some beer in her astonishment at his brazenness. She barely pulled the bottle from her mouth when his lips were on hers. He pulled away, momentarily reacquiring his senses, but Juanita seized the opportunity; throwing her arms around him she pressed herself against him.

Marion returned her embrace; they kissed long and deep. Their beverages tipped over spilling their contents onto the floor. He pulled her top off over her head; with abandon he suckled her soft firm mounds. Within moments they were wildly engaged in intercourse on the couch. Juanita expertly handled Marion's ardor bringing him easily to seventh heaven with her passionate touch.

"Where were you?" Martha demanded when the door opened and Marion stepped in.

"JESUS! What's with you?" Marion exclaimed in surprise when he saw her defiantly standing with hands on hips in the foyer.

"Where were you?" Martha repeated.

"With Jacques," Marion replied, walking away.

"Doing what?" she demanded.

"He wanted me to see some property; we drove to the south side of the island," Marion said, walking up the stairs.

"Really? Jacques, who was at the office all day?" she declared.

Marion paused at the top of the stairs, "You spoke to him?"

"No, I just called late this afternoon, and the girl who answered said he was on the phone and had been there all day."

"Well she was wrong," Marion shot back before turning and walking up the stairs.

"Don't turn your back on me!" she shouted, surprising herself when she heard her voice echoing off the walls. She stormed up the stairs behind him. Marion entered the washroom. A locked door met Martha.

"Open the door, Marion!"

Nothing . . . "Open the fuckin' door!" she yelled, violently shaking the doorknob.

Jacques picked up on the first ring when Juanita called him at home. "Ola?"

"It's me."

"Finally! What happened?" Jacques asked eagerly.

"I'm in," she informed him.

"You are? Did you . . .?"

"Yes."

"Yes what?"

"You know . . . we fucked."

"How was it, did he appear, how you say . . . impressed? Did he make the first move? Was he interested? Tell me everything," Jacques questioned eagerly.

"He did, he sort of caught me off guard—"

"How?" Jacques interrupted.

"Well, we came to my place, I changed into something casual, and I offered a drink . . ."

"Yes, yes, go on," Jacques prompted.

"He kissed me, and it went from there."

"So you fucked?"

"Yes. He left a little while ago. He seemed quite absorbed by our little escapade," she said confidently.

"Tell me everything," Jacques demanded.

Juanita paused. She was in no mood to recount her sexual acts in detail to him. She politely explained to Jacques that she was tired and wished to get to bed.

"But when are you seeing him again?" Jacques insisted.

"He said he'd call me. Don't worry, he will, they always do. Good night." With that she hung up.

Juanita was annoyed by the phone call. Jacques always used her services, and compensated her suitably by island standards, but she knew she would get only a pittance compared to what was up for grabs. She contemplated what would ensue and where it would lead from here. Would he pursue a relationship with her? Would he risk it all to be with her? These scenarios played in her head as she ran herself a bath.

Easing herself into the warm water, her thoughts turned to the afternoon's escapade. It had gone far smoother than she thought it would. She'd had no doubts that she would lure him to make a move on her, but she thought it was going to be harder than it had turned out to be. She was certain she had captivated him, since after he'd achieved satisfaction, once, twice, and again, he still stayed. He'd certainly wished to delay his departure; but finally had to excuse himself to reluctantly go home to his wife.

She found him quite competent in his lovemaking; she had to think long and hard to recall a more pleasant sexual experience. Their lovemaking started aggressive and then turned passionate. Tempering their ardour, he insisting on satisfying her needs first. She wasn't used to the attentiveness he showed towards her. He kissed and licked every inch of her body before settling on pleasing her orally. She was pleasantly surprised at how attentive he was in gratifying her. At first she intended to let him delight himself in this valiant act of manliness before she would dutifully turn the tables and show him some of her own talents; but she soon decided to let him run with the ball.

Sex had, over time, unfortunately become little more than a job for her. Her function was to please her clients, which were mostly older, time-sensitive men. The old "wham-bam, thank you ma'am" scenario was all too common. With Andrew, she had found herself letting her guard down. She decided against her usual routine of moaning and falsely complimenting her client for the prescribed duration, faking an orgasm, and quickly finishing him off. She lay back and relished Marion's dexterous tongue. Her moans were not feigned; she was actually relishing the sensations she was receiving from his attentions.

Moments later she found herself climaxing from the attention of another man, as opposed to achieving satisfaction by her own hand. With her lifestyle, sex was plentiful but gratification was not. A smile came across her beautiful face as she lathered her body while contemplating her rewarding day.

Jacques frowned after speaking with Juanita. They'd exploited his knowledge of clients' personal wealth and her ability to impress those same clients. However, this time she did not convey the same interest in the hunt that she had on other occasions. Was she becoming jaded? Was she tired after a marathon sexual encounter, or was she swayed by this younger prospect? He would have to monitor the situation closely.

Marion sat on the edge of the tub, relieved to hear Martha stomp away down the hall. And gratefully—at least she would be in no mood for sex. He was tapped out physically from the day's exhilarating marathon. With his head in his hands he questioned himself. What had gotten into him? Yes, Juanita was no doubt a stunningly beautiful woman, but what he had done was totally out of character. Actually putting the moves on a woman, throwing caution to the wind; he'd surprised himself. But the day's events had been more than worthwhile even with Martha alerted to something strange going on. He snapped himself out of his stupor and peeled off his clothes, tossing the lot into the hamper. Stepping into the shower, he washed in the hope of cleansing away every shred of evidence of his infidelity.

Martha lay in bed awake. She was aware of Marion getting into bed with her, but she didn't acknowledge him. He leaned over, kissing her on the cheek, and she shied away from his polite peck.

He whispered, "Tomorrow we'll spend the day together, I promise."

The following morning, Martha and Marion were being served breakfast on the patio; Martha was distant, avoiding all conversation. Marion had attempted to converse, but was ignored. Martha simply stared pensively at the horizon. Marion was thankful when the maid approached him with the cordless phone. He answered it, and a smile came across his face as he put his hand on the receiver.

"Honey, our car arrived. The dealer wants to know if we want delivery today."

He was thankful she acknowledged him, although Martha simply nodded her acceptance. Marion confirmed their willingness to accept delivery and hung up.

"I'll have the maid prepare us a picnic lunch; they're delivering our car within the hour," he declared with a wide grin.

Martha couldn't help but smile sheepishly before they went up to change. Marion took the opportunity to sit on the bed next to Martha and asked forgiveness for his being distant lately. Martha coolly nodded her absolution, and returned Marion's kiss.

The day was like so many others on the island paradise, hot, bright and pleasantly breezy. Martha sat in the passenger seat of their new acquisition, a silver Porsche 911 turbo. With Marion guiding the powerful, rumbling car down the winding island roads, Martha delighted in their new toy. She ran her hand over the glove leather seats, impressed by their soft, cushiony feel. She raised her arms up so she could feel the wind streaming through her open fingers, closing her eyes to the pleasant sensation. It reminded her of Sunday drives on hot summer days as a small girl, when she'd stick her arm out the car window and do aerodynamic stunts with her hand.

She relished the feeling of freedom. This was truly the first time she'd felt this liberated. She marvelled at Marion's skillful piloting of the gleaming Porsche, putting it through its moves expertly. The stunning landscape, combined with the stark mix of wealth and poverty that the island was reputed for, sped past. Men, women, children, old, young, all securing a day's wages that wouldn't even buy one of this car's lug nuts. She felt truly privileged.

Marion slowed to scout a small patch of white sand in a secluded cove. Rocky outcrops framed the secluded oasis. Marion parked on the gravel shoulder. When the engine's throaty rumble ceased, they were treated to the sound of the ocean breaking up on the rocks below. Marion retrieved the picnic basket with one hand, while grasping Martha's hand with the other. Both skipped over the worn, patchy grass path that led down to the ocean. Giggling like children, they slid down onto the sand. Marion quickly slipped off his shorts and top, and Martha did the same. Nude, both ran towards the welcoming water.

Martha, giggling, teased Marion. They frolicked freely in the warm, clear ocean water. Martha relished the sensation of the swirling water over her naked body. Marion held her tightly around her waist from behind before cupping a breast, his insistent erection pressing against her buttocks. Their gleeful laughter echoed off the cliffs behind them. She turned to face him, wrapping her legs around him, pulling him tightly to her. They kissed; Martha savoured the saltiness on their lips while Marion probed her entrance with his penis. She held onto him tightly as his member entered her. They made spontaneous love in the water with total abandon.

This day was the greatest in Martha's life. They had made love, then shopped, explored, and played like children. For the first time, Martha let herself be entirely enchanted by his uncharacteristic joviality. Marion had been charming and good-humoured, a side he'd not revealed before. They ended the day by stopping at the little cove they'd discovered earlier in the day. Sitting on the sand they observed a glorious, fiery sunset, romantically holding each other. Martha wondered if this was all a dream, while Marion wondered how wise it would be to see Juanita.

The next day, Martha awoke finding Marion dressing,

"Where are you going?" she asked sleepily.

"I have to meet with that land developer Jacques had introduced me to, to discuss a potential investment," he casually replied, fastening his belt.

"I'll come with you," Martha offered.

Casually, without making eye contact, he replied, "No, honey, it'll be a boring business meeting. Anyhow, I'll be back by this evening. We can meet him together if he has anything worthwhile to offer." He kissed her forehead before leaving.

She slipped on her robe covering her nudity before going out on the bedroom balcony to see Marion pulling away. Lisle's compact pickup pulled up just as Marion sped away. They politely honked a greeting as they passed one another. Lisle parked to the side of the wide, circular driveway and got out, stretching his shirtless frame. He saw Mrs. Margaret on the balcony and waved a greeting.

"Hi, Lisle, what's the plan for today?" Martha pleasantly asked.

"Cleaning the pool, then I'm going to town to pick up some supplies."

"Great! When you go, I'll come with you."

Lisle shrugged his shoulders, replying, "Certainly, Mrs. Margaret. It'll be a pleasure."

He found it odd that she would request to accompany him on his errands. He had no problems with her request; he only hoped Carlos wouldn't chastise him over it.

Marion pulled up in front of Juanita's place. The sound of the car's shrill horn reverberated off the surrounding buildings. Juanita dashed out. Getting into the car, she kissed Marion before complimenting him on his new acquisition. They pulled away, rumbling down the narrow street. Juanita fawned over Marion, her hand resting on his thigh.

"Where are you taking me?" she asked.

"You'll see," he replied.

Martha threw in her purse onto the truck's bench seat after Lisle had removed some clutter. The black vinyl seats scorched Martha's thighs when she sat. She grimaced a smile.

"Are you sure you want to come along, Mrs. Margaret?" Lisle cautioned.

"Yes! Of course! It'll be fun," she assured him.

"And call me by my nickname: Martha."

Lisle got behind the wheel after he'd secured her door. "Hold on tight, Mrs. Martha."

The bouncy, rattling truck was a far cry from yesterday's sophisticated transportation, but Martha was just happy to be out again. Yesterday had been a welcome respite from the monotony of luxurious living. Martha found Lisle refreshingly entertaining. A good ten years her junior, he exuded charm and self-confidence. He didn't display any of the subdued resentment many of the locals showed. His happy-go-lucky style was truly delightful to Martha; she'd noted this the moment she met him, when they first arrived.

"I'll just be a minute, Mrs. Martha," he said, pulling into a dirt parking lot.

"Wait. I want to come in too!" She hurriedly exited the truck's cab.

The front of the general store was lined with colourful baskets containing an assortment of products, including decorative bars of soap, T-shirts, and seashell souvenirs. Lisle took her hand and pulled her inside. Through hanging plastic beads they entered the shop. Martha paused a moment for her eyes to accustom to the comparative gloom.

"Mrs. Martha, this is my *hermana*, Rosa." He introduced her to a slight, very attractive young woman. The family resemblance was obvious.

The girl pleasantly smiled a greeting to her guest, advancing to kiss both her brother and Martha on the cheek. Martha blushed.

"My friends call me Martha."

"My sister runs the family business," Lisle informed her.

He then addressed his sister, "*Martha es mi jefa y buena amiga.*"

Rosa picked up a turquoise necklace from a display on the counter and fastened it around Martha's neck. "*Un obsequio para usted.*"

Martha, surprised at the offer of a gift, politely put her hand out in an attempt to decline.

"It's a gift for you," Rosa repeated in English, insistently looping it around her neck.

"It's beautiful! *Gracias.*" Martha smiled radiantly at Rosa while stroking the beads around her collar.

"*Su jefa es muy hermosa,*" Rosa said to Lisle coyly.

Lisle blushed, "*Lo sé, tengo mucha suerte.*"

"*Tenga cuidado*" the sister cautioned.

When they left, Martha asked if he'd drive down a certain road. She informed him that she thought she recognized the area; Lisle obliged. A short distance later, Martha spotted the place where she and Marion had been to the day before. To her surprise she saw their car parked on the side of the road at the same spot. "There! Stop there!" She pointed.

Pulling up behind the Porsche, Lisle parked his truck. Martha beamed not only with the excitement at having located their romantic cove, but also of finding Marion there. *Was he planning to buy the property as a surprise*? she wondered.

Her joy was short-lived when she spotted Marion walking on the beach holding hands with a voluptuous young woman. Lisle looked at Martha questioningly; Lisle quickly put two and two together, and put the truck in gear. Martha sat stunned, staring expressionlessly forward. Her eyes were moist but did not cry.

"I'll take you home," Lisle offered.

"No, I can't, just take me away from here, please," Martha begged.

Lisle acknowledged her request, pulling away.

He lived only a short distance away. Lisle parked in front of his modest cabana. He parked the truck and walked around to open Martha's door. Bashfully taking her hand, he helped her out of the truck. Martha hugged Lisle tightly, sobbing humbly. Lisle held her tight, patting her back in a caring attempt to comfort her.

Once inside, he sat her on the couch while he went to retrieve sodas from the fridge. Martha sat staring blankly at the floor; she was obviously distraught at what she'd seen. She tried to justify what she'd witnessed, but the facts were too obvious. Marion and this unknown woman were obviously holding hands and romantically strolling down the beach. The same beach they'd romantically made love on just the day before. Her fragile self-confidence, which she'd been nursing over the past few weeks, was quickly dissipating. She questioned if her love for him had been too hasty— after all she did barely know him. Her first impression of him was a negative one; he had grown on her out of necessity more than anything else. She did, however, love him. He had been an important ingredient in her betterment.

Martha was experiencing sensory overload; every negative emotion was fighting for supremacy: hatred, jealousy, fear, and betrayal. Lisle returned from the kitchen to find her sitting in a hunched-forward position on the couch, her hair cascading in unruly strands over her face. The one eye he could see was wet from crying; her bottom lip, like her body, trembled uncontrollably. He set the two soft drinks he was carrying back from the fridge down on the rattan coffee table before sitting next to Martha, his arm around her shoulders. Martha turned to look at him; her tear-streaked face was devoid of all emotion. Momentarily she looked into his eyes before leaning forward to kiss him.

Lisle returned her kiss, his eyes remaining open, questioning the wisdom of what was happening. Although he found her attractive and alluring, he also knew full well that what they were doing was inappropriate. His dissent was short lived when Martha eased him onto his back, and, sliding atop him she fumbled with his belt and zipper.

They had made love on the couch. Lisle lay back with Martha resting her head on his naked chest. All he could see of her was the top of her head, her right hand resting on his torso, and part of her rump. He did not know if she was awake and did not wish to disturb her. Running his hand through her tangled hair he kissed her head. Martha turned to look at him, propping her chin atop his athletic chest she looked at him wordlessly.

"I'm sorry," Lisle ventured.

Frowning slightly, Martha asked, "Sorry? For what?"

Pausing a moment, Lisle considered his reply before simply shrugging his shoulders. This innocent act prompted Martha to giggle. Lisle was pleased to see her smile.

Returning her head to his chest she said, "Oh Lisle, this is so fucked up. What am I going to do?"

Lisle reached for her chin, turning her face towards his. "You must speak to him, clarify the situation," he suggested.

Smiling at him, she stared wordlessly into his eyes before responding. Then she said, "I need to understand the situation first. What did I do wrong? Why would he do this?"

Then, in an attempt to boost her waning confidence she asked, "Do you find me attractive, Lisle?"

Taken aback by her bold question, he immediately replied, "Yes! Of course, very much so."

"Really? You're sure?" she reiterated.

Wordlessly Lisle lifted her chin, kissing her lips. Their tongues gently intermingled. He rolled Martha onto her back, kissing her passionately. Martha observed Lisle as he kissed his way along her neck, shoulders and breasts before continuing downward. Martha saw Lisle's face settle between her legs. With a gasp she threw her head back.

At sundown Martha asked Lisle to drive her home. She would have preferred to spend the night with Lisle; however, having been seen leaving with him, she realized it would not bode well for him if she did not return.

They were silent in the truck, Lisle staring forward at the road while Martha stared out her window blankly at the darkness. Driving through the town, Martha's attention was drawn to a metallic gleam on a side street. She immediately ordered Lisle to stop the truck and to reverse. He heeded her command, the truck reversed emitting a mechanical whine. She recognized their Porsche parked on a side street. She ordered Lisle to stop. Staring pensively at the car, she thought momentarily before exiting the truck.

Lisle begged her, "Get in Martha, let me drive you home."

Shouldering her bag, she said, "No . . . I'll walk a bit."

"Martha, please—"

"NO, go!" she commanded, slamming her door closed.

Sheepishly he conceded to her determination, reluctantly driving away.

Late that night Martha was still sitting behind the wheel of the parked Porsche. She played and replayed the day's events in her head while staring fixedly down the street. Thunder rolled in the distance; the air had the humid, electrified quality of an impending storm. The car's retracted top allowed gusts of wind to toss her hair about. She remained oblivious to all stimuli, staring ahead.

She had made love to Lisle earlier in a blend of vengeance and the desperate need for comfort. He obliged willingly, satisfying whatever need she had at that time. They had hardly spoken, both cognizant of the little assurance words would bring. She had counted on Marion being home by the time she returned, waiting and wondering where she was. She intended to hurt him by divulging her deed that day in order to humiliate him, as he had done to her. When she had spotted his parked car, she realized he wasn't at home dutifully waiting for her return. With her key in hand, she contemplated taking the car, leaving him stranded; but the situation warranted more than a childish prank—it justified a blatant confrontation.

In the late night, all was quiet on the narrow street. She sat wondering what was going on at this moment. Where was he exactly? Were they fucking? Of course they were. She imagined his mistress's mouth around his cock, her pussy on his face, the two laughing, teasing, kissing. All her suppositions served to fuel her developing madness.

She'd come a long way from being an abused, belittled, penniless housewife. The thought of being taken for a fool enraged her even further. She contemplated her actions when he would finally emerge, and the impending altercation served to heighten her state of mental distress.

Movement from down the street disrupted her troubled thoughts. Suddenly she perceived a shadow descending a dimly lit stairwell leading to the street. Marion appeared, distracted, fumbling with one hand in his pocket. Curtains parted in a second-floor window, and his new companion sweetly called down to him. Illuminated by the room's light, she could be seen holding a towel to her naked chest. Marion turned to look up, and smiled as she tossed the key ring down to him,

"You forgot your keys, my love."

Those words served to short-circuit what little capacity for rational thinking remained. Martha's ears rang loudly and her vision tunneled. All she saw now was Marion blowing a kiss to his lover after catching the keys and turning to cross the street to where his car was parked.

Martha turned the ignition key; the engine growled to life. Marion was starkly illuminated where he stood, looking ahead confused when he heard the unmistakable sound of his car's engine starting. In the car light's bright blue glare he squinted, and, shielding his eyes from the intense xenon lights, he peered forward in a moment of uncertainty.

Martha engaged the transmission, gunning the engine. The powerful sports car pounced forward, clipping the bumper of a car parked in front of her. A headlight burst under the impact, showering the pavement with sparks and glass. Marion, now illuminated by the one remaining light, stood frozen in shock.

Martha redirected the car with difficulty. She hadn't counted on the car's instantaneous, powerful response and before she realized it she was upon Marion, helplessly standing directly in her path. The car struck him violently and in the short distance it had travelled, the Porsche had already attained an astonishingly high rate of speed. Martha threw her arms up to shield her face, but not before her mind registered Marion's horror-stricken stare when the car impacted him. The remaining headlight shattered when the car struck him. Martha perceived a shadow race by above her head before she sideswiped another parked car, shearing off her driver's side mirror. Weaving down the road, she managed to regain control of the hell-bound sports car. She tore around the corner, tires screeching, clipping yet another parked car.

Juanita witnessed the frightful event from her second-floor window. It happened so quickly that she had no time to yell out a warning. She saw the Porsche peel away from the curb in a shower of sparks when it impacted the car parked before it. She momentarily registered Martha at the wheel just before the scene went black with the shattering of the remaining headlight. She stared in dismay at Marion's body somersaulting through the air before dropping in a limp mass onto the pavement. Her vision focused on his inanimate body lying in a grotesque, contorted heap. Immediately she ran down, unconcerned by her state of undress.

Martha ripped down an open stretch of road. She finally tuned in to the car's hair-trigger steering. Driving virtually blind, she followed the barely perceptible white line down the centre of the road. The occasional bolt of lightning from the approaching storm oriented her. Tears welling up in her eyes as well as the shattered windshield impeded her vision. Realizing what she'd done caused her to sob uncontrollably while she searched for a familiar landmark to guide her in her escape. She hadn't wished to run over Marion, she merely meant to scare him, teach him a lesson. Blind rage and unfamiliarity with the auto's performance combined to produce the disastrous results. She came upon the road that she recognized as stretching along the coast.

Juanita fell to her knees next to Marion as he lay on his back, eyes wide and staring blankly. His legs were bent under him, grossly distorted. His chest heaved spastically. She cried his name, slipping her arm under his neck and raising his head. Without acknowledging her, he spewed a massive quantity of blood from his gaping mouth. Rain started pelting down on them, streaking his blood down her naked torso. She screamed in horror while the life drained from her lover.

An incessant, urgent honking outside his cabana awakened Lisle. He jumped out of bed and peered out his window. Through the heavy downpour, he made out the silhouette of a convertible illuminated only by a single working parking light. He immediately ran out, finding Martha slumped over the steering wheel sobbing uncontrollably. Opening the driver's side door, he pulled her out of the idling car. She hugged him tightly, screaming,

"I killed him! Oh God, I killed him!"

Juanita sat in shock on the curb; a neighbour had wrapped a blanket around her while another attempted to shield her from the heavy downpour with an umbrella. A policeman crouched next to her, with a hand on her shoulder, trying to get a statement. Another officer contained the gathering crowd. Marion's lifeless body lay where he'd fallen, surrounded by a pinkish blend of blood and rainwater. An ambulance pulled up with lights flashing and siren blaring. The attendants rushed to examine Marion. Moments later, one of them retrieved a white sheet from the idling emergency vehicle and covered the body.

Martha trembled uncontrollably in Lisle's arms as he tried to calm her. Sitting on the couch where only hours before they had been making love, she stared fixedly at the floor, finally revealing to Lisle what transpired.

"I killed him, I ran him over. I didn't mean to. I didn't mean to. I didn't mean to," she repeated incessantly.

"Are you sure he's dead?" Lisle managed to ask.

"He must be. How could he not be?" she responded.

In the predawn hours, Lisle drove the damaged Porsche through the rain. He planned to abandon it as discreetly as possible. He knew of a secluded road leading to the coast. He squinted at the darkness till he arrived at an embankment. There he stopped. The night was inky black and only the occasional lightning burst broke the darkness. He exited the idling car, leaving it in "drive," and scouted the area before releasing the handbrake. The car lumbered forward, picking up speed down the embankment. He stared at the rear lights bouncing over the uneven terrain before disappearing over the cliff's edge. Moments later, he heard a dull splash from below. Turning, he ran through the heavy rain all the way home.

Martha sat, still in shock, and trembling. She wore one of Lisle's sweaters to warm her. Her soaked clothing was discarded on the floor. He'd suggested they dump the car in an attempt to throw off the authorities. Reluctantly Martha agreed to the improvised ruse. Lisle had convinced her that passing off what had happened as a regrettable accident would not fly. In a moment of lucidity she agreed. She'd stay with him till she could formulate a plan of action.

Chapter 15

Inspector Linton looked down the steep embankment to the surf below. The children that spotted the wreck were being interviewed by one of his constables. He eyed the car from above. It rested on its side in about five feet of water. In his mind he scrutinized the scene: car, but no body; the night before was high tide. The car would have plunged into eight, maybe ten feet of water at the time. If she'd been at the wheel she could conceivably have been swept out to sea. However, the waves are high on the north side of the island. If there were a body, it would most probably have washed up on one of the rock outcroppings.

A boat was patrolling the coast for five miles in either direction in the event there was a body to be found.

"Hell of a night, Inspector," a voice said from behind him.

Inspector Linton turned to see his colleague, Inspector Bonneau, standing behind him.

"Yes, that it was," Linton confirmed before turning back to peer out over the ocean.

"If anyone drove it off the cliff from this height, they're surely dead," Bonneau speculated.

"And if anyone pushed it off, they picked the perfect night for it," Linton stated pensively.

"Really? And why is that?" Asked Bonneau.

"Heavy rain until this morning . . . Washed away any footprints," Linton stated.

"I must show up for work," Lisle insisted.

"Please don't go. I don't want to be alone," Martha begged.

"If I don't show, someone may come here. Besides, once at your house I'll know what they know," Lisle reasoned.

Martha conceded to his logic.

"Listen, there's some money at the house—I'll need it. Around twenty-five thousand dollars is in the safe. You must retrieve it."

"Where? How can I—" Lisle protested.

Martha placed a finger to his lips, "I can kiss the fortune goodbye, but I must have that money if I stand any chance of making it off this island. Please help me," she pleaded.

Lisle nodded his commitment.

"In the entrance closet, behind the shoe rack there is a wall safe. Here's the combination." She handed him a slip of paper. Lisle took the note, kissed her, and left.

Martha flushed, watching Lisle pull away from the house. Once again she had put her trust in a man, a virtual stranger no less. What would stop him from pocketing the money and coming back with the authorities? Had she ever not been betrayed and abused by every man she'd come across in her life? What would stop this kid, holding practically a lifetime's worth of wages in his hand, from turning her in? How could she have been so stupid?

But what choice did she have? She trembled with anxiety. Should she run? Where? How? She had only the clothes on her back. She started resigning herself to her fate. Surely she would go to jail, unless the authorities would believe her version that it was all an unfortunate mistake. A crime of passion . . . Yes, a crime of passion; she'd been jilted, her husband cheated on her, abused her trust. Maybe she could simply be deported back home and face a court that could comprehend her situation. After all, she still had her money, she could surely afford a good lawyer. That last thought served to convince her to cut her losses and run.

Lisle pulled up to Martha's villa. An unfamiliar car was parked out front. Lisle began to perspire when he concluded that it was surely the police. He parked as he would usually. When he exited his pickup, a man in a suit approached him from the house.

"Ramirez? Lisle Ramirez?" the paunchy middle-aged man inquired.

Throwing a coiled vacuum hose over his shoulder Lisle answered, "Yes?"

Flipping his lapel over to show a badge, the man introduced himself: "Detective Linton. Could you please follow me inside to answer a few questions?"

Lisle's mind raced. "Yes, of course. Is anything wrong?"

"Yes actually, very much so," he answered.

Lisle realized he'd scarcely planned for this. He'd hoped to find only the butler and maid at the house, and didn't really expect a detective. Lisle decided to tell him the truth to a point.

Once Lisle set the hose back in the truck he followed the detective inside the house. Entering, he eyed the entrance closet where Martha told him he would find the wall safe. He still couldn't fathom how he'd access it without being detected. From down the hall he saw Carlos the butler and Susanna the maid sitting in the dining room; both sat mournfully. Susanna's eyes were red from crying, a handkerchief still in her hand. Another man, surely a detective as well, sat scribbling notes in a pad. All of the participants eyed him, but none spoke. Detective Linton showed Lisle into the parlour, courteously leading him by his arm.

Taking a seat in one of two identical wing chairs, the detective invited Lisle to be seated across from him in the other.

"What's going on?" Lisle asked.

"I need to ask you a few questions first, Mr. Ramirez," the detective stated.

"Yes, go on," Lisle said agreeably.

"When did you last see your employers, Mr. and Mrs. Finley?"

"Yesterday," Lisle answered, appearing as perplexed as he could.

"Go on," Linton prompted.

"I saw Mr. Finley yesterday morning about nine; I was pulling up to the house and he was leaving."

"Continue," Linton encouraged.

Lisle went on to relate the day's events as relatively normal except for the fact that Mrs. Margaret asked him to give her a lift into town, which he did. After shopping for a few things and accompanying him on a few errands, they were driving back through town when she asked him to drop her off.

"What time was this?" Linton asked.

Lisle hesitated in his reply, if he'd tell him the real time Linton would want a detailed account of what they'd done all that time. Lisle had no intention of having him realize that he and his employer fucked the afternoon away. He told him he dropped her off mid-afternoon.

After seemingly satisfying Linton in his quest for clues, Lisle seemed off the hook. Linton thanked him for his time, and gave his blessing for Lisle to go about his chores. Before taking his leave, Lisle asked what all this was about.

Linton eyed him momentarily.

"Mr. Finley was killed last night, seemingly by his wife. We suspect she then committed suicide."

Lisle looked shocked, surprised by the suicide remark.

"How? Where? Here?" Lisle bombarded Linton with questions.

Raising his hand Linton simply stated, "I'm sure you'll be brought up to date by the other staff once we've finished interviewing them."

Lisle stepped outside and went about his routine; he felt he'd handled the interrogation well. Now he needed to buy time till he could access the money in the safe. From the rear of the house where he tended to the pool he heard car doors close before driving away. Lisle worked slowly, hoping for a chance to get into the house. Just when he'd convinced himself it was futile, Carlos came out onto the terrace, pausing to run his hands through his hair and down his face; he looked exhausted.

"Carlos, what's this all about?" Lisle asked innocently.

Carlos waved away Lisle's question, "I'll tell you when I get back. Susanna's not feeling well and asked me to drive her home. Can you stay till I return?"

"Yes, of course," Lisle assured him.

"You'll find drinks and snacks in the refrigerator, if you like," Carlos informed him before walking around the side of the house to retrieve his car.

Lisle couldn't believe his good fortune. The matter of how he'd enter the house to retrieve the money had plagued him. He normally had no reason to enter the house. As a matter of fact, today was the first time he'd gone into it. Even when he needed to use the washroom, he'd go to the small pool house, but never the villa. Hearing Carlos pull away, Lisle ran to the front of the house to assure himself he was alone.

Inside the house, he went straight to his objective. Opening the closet he was relieved to spot the shoe rack Martha had spoken of. He pulled forward on it but it did not budge. Panicked, he rattled, shook, and twisted the wood shelving. Shoes tumbled to the floor in the process. After a seemingly interminable lapse of time, the section finally swung aside; he'd simply been pulling on the wrong side in his desperate attempt to move it. The wall safe was revealed. Retrieving the paper Martha had scribbled the combination on, he proceeded to dial the series of numbers: two left turns . . . 5 . . . one right . . . 37 . . . then 17.

He sighed audibly when the handle moved with an audible click. Opening the door, he found some papers and a thick envelope. The envelope contained the cash Martha had assured him would be there. He pulled out all the contents before closing the thick door, replaced the scattered shoes, and made his way out of the house. Lisle waited anxiously for Carlos to return. He was eager to get back to Martha.

Lisle had not returned. Martha rode in the passenger seat of the rusty old dump truck that had graciously stopped to pick her up as she hitchhiked. Contemplating her fate, she'd decided to turn herself in. In her state of paranoia, she'd convinced herself that Lisle had likely pocketed the money and was turning her in to the police. She'd been unable to deal with her guilt during the past few hours of solitary confinement. She was going to turn herself in to Jacques and suffer the inevitable consequences of her actions. She mistrusted Jacques as much as anyone else at this point, but knew no one else on the island that could help her. She hoped he would lessen the wrath of the authorities through his influence.

Jacques sat with his hand to his forehead incredulously listening to his office radio. Juanita hadn't shown up for work and he'd been unable to reach her. The morning news recounted the night's tragic events:

"Police are investigating a dramatic hit-and-run incident which occurred last night at 11:20 p.m. in the central district of San Liborio on Sosua Street. A man was struck down in the street by a car presumably driven by his wife. Preliminary information points to a lover's triangle involving another woman. The victim, identified as Andrew Finley, died at the scene of his injuries sustained when the driver of a silver convertible hit him at high speed. No one else was injured in the incident; however, the second woman, who at this time remains unidentified, is in hospital recovering from shock. Witnesses say the unidentified woman, who witnessed the incident, was found in the nude holding the victim when help arrived. Police are still waiting for her account once her condition improves. The vehicle involved was found early this morning in the surf; it had been driven off a cliff. The body of the driver has not yet been recovered, but a search is currently underway. Anyone with information in this case is asked to contact the police."

Jacques grabbed his jacket and left for the hospital. He'd just unlocked his car door when a large truck pulled up beside him. Looking up, he was astonished to see Martha looking down at him.

"Jacques, I need your help," she informed him.

Lisle was listening to the radio in the truck on his way home. In his attempt to dispose of the vehicle, he'd not even considered it would be perceived as a suicide. It had not been a stroke of genius but a total fluke that authorities would suppose this. He sped up, wondering if Martha knew any of the developments. He pulled up to his home and rushed in to find it empty.

Jacques looked around nervously before quickly pulling her out of the truck. He ushered her into his car. There, he asked what had happened. Martha cried uncontrollably, between sobs recounting the fateful episode. Jacques' mind quickly analyzed the situation, and with steely deliberation quickly came up with a plan to profit from the situation.

"Listen to me carefully," he instructed before proclaiming his plan of action.

Juanita lay on the hospital bed in a total state of shock. She'd been sedated and was resting; however, she had not spoken since the events of the previous night. A policeman sat in the room with instructions to call investigators when she'd regained her senses. They needed to hear her version of the events in order to fill in the blanks. All they had till now was based on assumption. All they knew was that the victim's wife had struck him down, but nothing else. The detectives were counting on Miss Mendosa to enlighten them.

The officer was sitting and quietly reading the paper when he heard a knock on the hospital room door. He stood and went to open it. Jacques stood there with a bouquet of flowers in hand and a concerned look on his face. The officer inquired what he wanted, and Jacques respectfully asked if he could see Juanita. The policeman informed him that the young woman was unresponsive and hadn't spoken since the incident. Jacques contained his pleasure at hearing the good news, and asked the officer if he could try to get her to speak, being a good friend and her employer. The guard shrugged, seeing no harm in his trying, and in taking the opportunity to stretch his legs a bit. He agreed to give Jacques a few minutes alone with her.

Jacques seized the opportunity as soon as the man closed the door behind him. Setting the flowers down, he shook Juanita as gently as the time constraint permitted. Juanita's eyes fluttered, soon she was staring at Jacques, confused and disoriented.

"Juanita, Juanita . . . wake up," he said softly.

Juanita took his hand and squeezed, but the sedatives distorted her perception; she simply asked, "Jacques?"

"Yes, Yes, it's me, Jacques. Wake up, we must talk." He took a glass of water from her bedside and wet her face with some droplets, which he sprinkled with his fingers. Juanita reacted to his stimulation, opening her eyes wide.

"Juanita, what happened?" he asked.

Juanita, lifting herself up in order to raise her head, began recounting the events of the night before. The sedative she'd been given appeared effective, in that she narrated the circumstances with little emotion, giving Jacques a good understanding of how it had played out.

"Have you told this to the police?" he asked, measuring his words.

"No, I don't think so . . . no, it was all too disturbing," she said slowly.

"Good, excellent, all is not lost, we can turn this unfortunate event in our favor. Juanita, look at me and listen very carefully."

Jacques recounted his plan; Juanita listened as intently as the drugs allowed her to, nodding often to confirm her understanding. Shortly after, the officer guarding Juanita called his superiors, informing them that his ward was capable of giving a statement now.

Jacques was back at his home, a pleasant house where he lived alone. Far from being impressive, it was still considered a grand home. The two-storey white stucco and red brick dwelling was situated in the town centre on a boulevard a few blocks from the bank. The short driveway could accept only one car, and the whole property was surrounded by an eight-foot wrought iron fence, accessible only through the main gate. He opened the door to find Martha sitting exactly where he'd left her a little over an hour ago. Martha looked at him warily as he walked towards her.

"I spoke with the girl, Juanita, who saw the accident."

"You mean the whore my husband was with," she corrected.

Jacques raised his hand and lowered his head in a show of complacency,

"I understand, but this girl is willing to modify, shall we say, her version of the events in order to minimize your responsibility."

"How?" Martha asked suspiciously.

"This is what she'll say and it's very important your version matches hers exactly," Jacques said before continuing.

The detectives looked at one another after Juanita gave her rendition of the night's events. Both were bewildered by her recital of what transpired. Circumstances pointed to another theory, but her version was plausible, too. The lead detective asked Juanita several times if she was certain of what she was declaring. Her reply was always yes. Both closed their note pads before taking their leave.

"Everything is as you say it happened," Jacques dictated to Martha, "except for the following: You saw his car parked and assumed he was close by, so you decided to sit in it and wait for him. You waited, not knowing where exactly he was or what he was doing. You never suspected he was cheating on you. Understood?"

Martha confirmed her understanding with a nod before he continued.

"Then you saw him leaving a building being bade farewell by a naked woman standing in an upstairs window. Is that fairly correct?"

Martha nodded in agreement.

"You then started the car," he continued, "and decided to leave him stranded. To your surprise, he bolted into the street in an attempt to stop you when he realized you saw everything." Jacques paused so Martha could absorb the information.

"Being angry, you accelerated in an attempt to get away, BUT . . . he bolted into the street in front of you, waving for you to stop. You struck a parked car when you swerved in an attempt to avoid him but unfortunately you struck him ACCIDENTALLY. In your panic you kept driving. Later in a fit of desperation you dumped the car over a cliff in your grief and distress." Martha listened expressionless.

"Today, repentant and grieving, you turned yourself in to me with a plea for understanding and assistance."

Martha contemplated what Jacques related to her.

"But I didn't mean to kill him."

"Maybe not, but your actions point to intent. This is why your version has to avoid showing this. It must impart no maliciousness on your part," Jacques explained.

"This girl—" Martha paused.

"Juanita," Jacques clarified.

"Juanita . . . She'll corroborate this?"

"Yes, absolutely," Jacques confirmed. "Now you must understand her cooperation and subsequent testimony comes at a price."

Martha, raising an eyebrow, waited for him to continue.

"Half of your assets," he stipulated.

Martha slumped in her seat, stunned. Before she could reply, Jacques added, "Without her cooperation you will surely go to prison, possibly for life."

Martha put her hands to her face and nodded in agreement.

Detective Linton was called to the lobby of the police station. There he found a suited black man with his arm around the shoulders of a pitiful-looking woman.

"Inspector Linton?" the black man asked.

"Yes," Linton confirmed.

"This is Margaret Finley, Andrew Finley's widow."

Linton raised his eyebrows in surprise before escorting them both into his office.

Once in Linton's office, he called to halt the ongoing search for her body. He then advised Margaret of her rights, which Jacques, as an advisor, said she was willing to waive. Linton listened intently to her version of the events, taking care to tape-record her confession. Once that was done, he placed her in custody till a judge could hear her declaration.

Lisle sat at home, clutching the envelope containing the money. He was at a loss as to Martha's whereabouts and to why she had left. He decided to tune in on the news hoping for an update on the situation. He didn't have long to wait; it seemed Martha had turned herself in to the authorities and was presently in custody awaiting a preliminary bail hearing.

Chapter 16

Three weeks later . . .

Martha was relieved it was over. The trial had gone relatively smoothly; she'd not been tried for murder, as she'd feared. That charge was never levied against her, following Juanita's deposition. She'd simply been found guilty of a hit-and-run accident, causing death. Her sentence was limited to a hefty fine, thanks to Juanita's testimony and her willingness to pay for all damages caused. She now sat at home alone and contemplated her life from this point on. Lisle had repeatedly tried to contact her, wanting to know what to do with the money he was holding, as well as desperately wanting to see her. However, she chose to avoid him throughout the trial period. Now that it was over, she allowed him to come over before she fulfilled her decision to pull up anchor. To where? She had no idea.

One thing Martha wanted to do before anything else was meet Juanita. She'd seen and heard her during her courtroom testimony, but she wanted to sit down and speak with her. She noticed during the trial that Jacques was very careful to keep them apart. Martha imagined it was to maintain protocol; it would be against everyone's interest if they appeared to communicate with one another. But now that it was over she'd like to see her and speak with her.

The doorbell rang; being home alone, she rose to answer it. Lisle stood before her, his hand holding an envelope stretched out to her. He looked helpless with his sad, puppy dog eyes staring back at her. She smiled and embraced him, hugging him tightly.

"I'm sorry I doubted you," she confessed.

"Why did you ignore me all this time? I don't understand."

"I didn't want to drag you down—you'd done enough for me, and my gratitude was to doubt you." Releasing her hold, she held him at arm's length. "I'm sorry."

She took his free hand and led him inside and up to her bedroom. There, whatever anxiety Lisle had suffered, she soon freed him of. She made love to him, feeling that again she'd skirted a tragedy. Her juices flowed with adrenaline as she took the young man totally. Lisle writhed beneath her, ecstatic with passion for this woman. Age difference, money, social standing were irrelevant to him; he simply wanted to be with her.

After their lovemaking, Martha, propped up on her elbows, stared at Lisle who was resting on his back. "What do you want from me, Lisle?" she ventured.

Surprised by her bold question, he looked at her, puzzled. "I don't want anything from you. I just want to be with you," he declared sincerely.

"I'm leaving this island. I'm resolving some details and leaving . . . forever."

"Take me with you," Lisle proposed.

Rolling onto her back, Martha laughed wholeheartedly. Lisle looked at her somberly. He wanted to be with her, help her, love her. Her breasts jiggled with her laughter, her belly trembled with her chuckles. Lisle rolled onto her, taking hold of her.

"Don't tease me. Don't I mean anything to you?" he pleaded.

She stopped laughing to look into his eyes; she noted the sincerity in them. Something she now realized she never saw in Marion's eyes and had certainly never seen in Hank's dead fish eyes. She wrapped her legs around his torso and held him tight.

"You have no idea who I am. How do you know I'm not a killer? A black widow?"

He returned her reflective gaze.

"I don't care. You may never be mine, but I'll always be yours." Gently he slid into her; she closed her eyes and sighed, accepting him willingly.

Against his better judgment, Lisle agreed to drive her to Juanita's place. Martha was adamant about speaking with her. Not out of anger or contemptuous motives, but to close that chapter of her life. She'd buried Marion under a headstone that read his alias; she knew she couldn't live with that thought. She'd promised herself and him she would write to his family confessing all that occurred over the brief time they'd been together. She wished to close all issues and start anew.

When they arrived on Juanita's street, Martha prepared herself for an emotional blow, which never came. She truly felt distanced from the woman who, out of weakness, reacted desperately and killed her husband. She had Lisle wait in the truck, assuring him she'd be back shortly.

Juanita opened her door to see Marion's wife standing before her. Juanita was at a total loss for words; in her doorway was her rival who'd precipitated the whole catastrophic incident.

"May I speak with you?" Martha asked.

Juanita stepped aside, wordlessly inviting her in. Once inside, both sat in the living room across from each other.

"I can see why Marion was attracted to you. You're very beautiful," Martha commented.

"Thank you. I hadn't wished things to be as they turned out to be," Juanita confessed.

"Did you love my husband?"

"I'm not sure, but I liked him very much. More than others I've known," she stated pensively.

"Why did you agree to testify in my favour? Was it for the money?"

Juanita lowered her head, staring at the floor.

"Yes . . . well, no… Jacques thought it would be for the best," she explained.

"Are you sleeping with Jacques?" Martha asked bluntly.

Juanita looked at her flabbergasted.

"GOD, NO!" She responded.

With tears in her eyes, Juanita confessed her association with Jacques, and how he matched up Marion and her with the intent of getting to the money. Martha listened intently to her side of the story. She soon came to the conclusion that this girl was not in herself evil, but a victim of circumstances much like herself. Martha soon determined that Juanita only used what God had given her for the purpose of bettering her life.

"How much is Jacques paying you for having testified in my favor?" Martha inquired.

"I'm . . . I'm not sure I should be discussing this with you," Juanita countered.

"Do you know how much Jacques asked of me?" Martha questioned.

"No, I don't," Juanita answered.

"Four million dollars."

Juanita's jaw dropped. "Four . . . Million . . . Dollars!"

Martha nodded in confirmation.

Juanita sheepishly confessed, "He promised me five thousand dollars."

Lisle breathed a sigh of relief when he saw Martha make her way back to the truck. Closing the door once inside, she turned to Lisle, "Are you sure you love me?"

With total sincerity he nodded.

"Are you sure you want to be with me, no matter what?"

Taking her hand, he squeezed it against his chest. "Yes," was all he said.

"Then let's go, there's much to be done."

Martha had Lisle drive her to the bank; there she met with Jacques.

"Margaret, my dear, what a surprise!" he cheerfully greeted her.

Martha had gone over to his office to discuss his payment. Jacques assured Martha that there was plenty of time, but since she was there, they could discuss the money transfer. Jacques informed her that in order to avoid suspicion, he was going to register a company in which she would invest the four million dollars, and he would then take it from there. He assured her that he'd committed most of the funds to others that aided her in her trial, ensuring there would be no conviction.

"Like Juanita?" Martha offered.

"Yes, Juanita, definitely. She was a key player, and much of the money is destined for her. She was very difficult to convince." Jacques flashed his patent, sickly grin.

"Where is she? I was hoping to thank her personally for her help."

"Oh, no, no, no. She's on a short sabbatical. She's still quite distraught and wouldn't appreciate being approached, and certainly not by you. No, I'll take care of things with Juanita."

"Fine, let me know when all is set up," Martha said, standing up.

"Certainly, not to worry. It is a small island—people cannot disappear easily, my dear," Jacques reminded her, chuckling; however, his eyes weren't smiling.

Once out of the bank, Martha, together with Lisle, left to set up her planned strategy. Lisle proved to be a worthy and much-appreciated ally in that endeavour. He knew many locals who were in a position to assist in their exodus.

The island that had served as her home over the past few months shrank in the distance as the ship sailed away from it. Martha stood on the rear deck watching the coast recede into the morning mist. The island was cloaked to its mountain peaks in haze. She came to the realization of how clouds formed while watching the encroaching heat raise the island's misty cloak skywards, revealing its protégé beneath before drifting skyward and away. Pensively she reflected on her brief existence there, her hair tousled about her face by the ocean breeze. She felt no attachment and experienced no regrets in choosing to leave. When she'd won the money she had viewed it as deliverance, but it had since then proved to be a magnet for trouble.

Slipping his arm around her waist and planting a kiss on her temple, Lisle joined her. Wordlessly she nestled her head on his chest, welcoming his loving touch. Together they were headed for a South American country that would afford sanctuary and hopefully an opportunity for yet another new life. She clutched her handbag containing all she needed to confirm her identity: bank documents and proofs of deposit as well as the money Lisle had retrieved. They had all they needed to commence anew. She had no intention of fulfilling her commitment to Jacques, especially since she discovered he'd precipitated the tragic events. She did, however, drop a letter into the mail before boarding addressed to Juanita and informing her that more than her promised share would be forwarded to her in the hope she would wisely use it, like herself, to better her existence.

Lisle had arranged for their flight by ship through a close friend who skippered the commercial vessel they were on and would take them discreetly to their new home. She had decided to avoid the option of flying out, recalling the friendly and influential way Jacques had spoken with the customs and immigration officers when they had first arrived.

Once they docked at their new destination, Martha would have her money transferred, in the hope of living a peaceful, secluded life with her new mate.

Conclusion

Hank Sr. sat together with Jackie, rocking peacefully on their front porch, her head resting on his shoulder as they sipped lemonade. The house had evolved into a home; it had been repainted in blue and white. The lawn was well tended and lush, and flowers—not weeds—grew in abundance in the flowerbeds. At their feet lay a dog they'd recently adopted after visiting a local animal shelter.

Hank Sr. had resisted taking in the mutt, but Jackie convinced her mate to become a master. He'd never seen a use for a dog; not in the city, anyway. However, when he saw the immediate connection between the beagle/terrier mix and his love, Jackie, he was driving the dog home not an hour later. He'd done it for Jackie, but now he and the dog had developed an inseparable relationship. Mac followed him step by step throughout the day. Hank Sr. couldn't help but smile when he looked at his faithful companion.

Hank Sr. had obsessed about the loss of the fortune with which Martha had disappeared, but time, love, and devotion had curbed his wrath and thirst for revenge. He no longer simply existed, but lived his life to the fullest, sharing what he had with his loving companion.

Jackie sat content with one hand on her growing belly. Hank Sr. received the news of his becoming a father with joy and anticipation. She was delighted with the turn for the better her life had taken. She had found her soul mate in the most unlikely of circumstances, and was now living out her life as she had always dreamed she would.

Jacques sat at his desk despondent and angry. His bank had just made an international transfer of over eight million dollars. He'd tried to stop the process, but try as he may, he was unable to contest or hold back the inevitable transaction. He now realized his plans of acquiring the small fortune were not to be. His greed was once again his undoing; nonetheless, his narrow-mindedness didn't allow for him to discern his errors. She would probably not have blinked at forking over a few hundred thousand dollars, or maybe even a million—but he had demanded half her wealth. He'd simply pulled too hard on the rope, and it had broken. Juanita was nowhere to be found, as well. She'd seemingly disappeared into thin air. He was certain she was involved in Martha's plan of leaving the island with her wealth.

Jacques wasn't one to believe in coincidences, but Martha's flight and Juanita's disappearance were too much to ignore. He had taken the precautions of alerting his contacts in immigration and various other vocations that would have been aware of any attempt on Martha's part to leave the island, but somehow she had slipped through his fingers unnoticed.

He never suspected in the slightest that Juanita would run as well. After all, he owed her money: Why would she? But she did; booked a flight, paid cash, and now was gone.

He now realized she had been a major asset in his various scams; years of preparation and grooming were gone. Just then Carla brought in his mail, and he was momentarily distracted from his sulking. He observed the diminutive young girl deposit a batch of envelopes held together by thick elastic. She smiled wordlessly at him before turning and exiting his office. He cocked his head, watching her leave; her hips, although shrouded beneath a long skirt, swayed provocatively. For months she'd been a clerk at the bank, yet he never had given her a second glance. He did need a new personal assistant. *She needs some work, but certainly has potential*, he thought.

Juanita returned to her native village with the one hundred thousand dollars Martha had wired her. Martha had offered her the large amount at their meeting in gratitude for her welcome testimony, but Juanita had never thought she'd actually follow through. She fully intended to use the money to set her life on the right track. All her adult life had been spent scraping a living while others exploited her beauty. Now, thanks to Martha's help, she had the tools and means to better her life.

Martha and Lisle sat on their section of private beach bordering their new home as they peacefully viewed the sun preparing to set. Martha finally had what she'd always hoped for: a caring and loving man, a real home, and a life worth living for. Lisle proved not only to be a dependable ally, but also a loving, caring, attentive man. With his hand on her belly, he delighted at the movement of the new life growing within her.

Fin

To order more copies of

UNPREDICTABLE
COMBINATIONS

By TIA DORÉ

Contact:

GENERAL STORE
PUBLISHING HOUSE

499 O'Brien Road, Box 415
Renfrew, Ontario Canada K7V 4A6
Telephone: 1-800-465-6072
Fax: (613) 432-7184
www.gsph.com

VISA and MASTERCARD accepted.

WOWZONE.COM/TIADORE